DEATH IN THE GARDEN . . .

"It's extraordinary." Marcel's voice beside me was hushed, almost reverential. Then he smiled. "And very romantic." He bent slowly toward me, cupped his hand under my chin, and lifted my face. I knew he was going to kiss me, and my heart was beating like mad. Suddenly I felt impossibly shy. I glanced away, down toward the water.

And then I screamed.

There was a body floating facedown among the lilies.

A Scent
of Murder

by Elizabeth Howard

illustrated by
Michael Wm. Kaluta

A BYRON PREISS BOOK

RANDOM HOUSE NEW YORK

Library of Congress Cataloging-in-Publication Data:
Howard, Elizabeth. A scent of murder.
(My name is Paris) "A Byron Preiss book."
SUMMARY: Sixteen-year-old Paris MacKenzie continues her adventures in Paris, France, when she discovers a body on the estate of the famous painter Claude Monet. [1. Mystery and detective stories. 2. Monet, Claude, 1840–1926—Fiction. 3. France—Fiction] I. Kaluta, Michael William, ill. II. Title. III. Series: Howard, Elizabeth. My name is Paris. PZ7.H8327Sc 1987 [Fic] 87-4583
ISBN: 0-394-87548-6 (trade); 0-394-97548-0 (lib. bdg.)

Manufactured in the United States of America 1 2 3 4 5 6 7 8 9 0

Special thanks to Michael Hardwick, Mollie Hardwick, Stephanie Spinner, Janet Schulman, Ellen Steiber, Tisha Hamilton, and Joan Brandt.

Book design by Alex Jay
Cover design by Alex Jay
Cover painting by Michael Wm. Kaluta
Edited by Ruth Ashby

MY NAME IS PARIS is a trademark of Byron Preiss Visual Publications, Inc.

MY NAME IS
PARIS

CHAPTER 1

"Look!" I cried. "A giant jellyfish!"

I pointed to a strange wooden sculpture, about five feet high. It had a large, dome-shaped head, supported by wavy stems that looked to me like tentacles.

"Hmmm." Beside me Marcel Fleury peered at the printed notice underneath the sculpture and smiled. "Not that I like to disagree with you, Paris, but apparently it's meant to be a music stand."

"Are you sure?"

"I'm sure," he replied. "I think it's the sculptor who's confused. As a jellyfish it makes sense. As a music stand it's simply absurd."

We were at the Grand Exposition of 1900—a vast city of colorful

3

pavilions that sprawled across both banks of the river Seine in Paris. We'd spent the afternoon wandering through displays of the latest wonders in science, industry, and fashion. Now we were in a pavilion devoted to artworks and furnishings in the new style known as Art Nouveau.

Ahead of me Marcel moved restlessly to the next exhibit. "You're not very keen on all of this, are you?" I said.

Marcel frowned. "I don't like to see chairs and tables and ironwork distorted by all these writhing vegetable forms."

I smothered a laugh as half the people in the pavilion turned to glare at him.

We were standing before a display of wineglasses shaped like tulips. Delicate green leaves branched out from their stems. "These are lovely," I ventured.

"Not very practical."

"No, but they remind me of similar ones in Uncle Claude's collection."

Exactly twenty-eight days ago I'd come to France, intending to spend a year with my uncle Claude. But on the day I arrived, my uncle was found dead—murdered in his study. A number of very strange things had happened immediately after; one of the strangest was learning that the uncle I'd never met had willed me most of his property. It was still hard to believe that at the age of sixteen I had my own townhouse in Paris, complete with servants, a car, and a small but distinguished collection of Art Nouveau and Impressionist works.

"Come on," Marcel said, taking my hand. "Let's go outside."

We made our way through the fairgrounds toward the benches by the riverbank. The late afternoon sun was glistening on the Seine and a sailboat drifted past us; two children on board waved madly at whoever would wave back. Couples and families strolled by, and then a group of what had to be six sisters, each carrying a parasol that matched her dress perfectly. We sat on one of the benches, saying nothing, just enjoying what was all around us.

For about the ninetieth time that day I found myself staring at Marcel, amazed that I'd been lucky enough to meet him. Marcel Fleury was twenty-one, a student at the Institute for Chemical Research, devastatingly handsome, and the main reason I was now nearly fluent in French. He was also my best friend. Since the day we'd met, when I was investigating my uncle's death, we'd had a kind of unspoken understanding—that he and I were on the same side. What we hadn't quite worked out was what else we had besides friendship. I knew he liked me, but I couldn't believe he liked me as much as I liked him.

"Now, *this* is art," he said.

"What is?"

He turned to me, smiling. "Sitting here with

you, watching the river go by."

I felt myself blushing. Back home in Chicago, the boys never said anything like that.

"It's just the kind of scene your friend Monet might paint," he went on.

"My friend?"

"Well, Paris, it's not everyone who has an original Monet hanging in the drawing room." He meant the painting that had been Uncle's most treasured possession. It was an oil, about four feet square, that showed a wooden Japanese-style bridge arching over a stream filled with water lilies. Every time I looked at it, I felt as if I'd entered some cool green paradise. "Monet is probably the greatest painter alive," Marcel continued.

"Uncle thought so too." I recalled a particularly long letter to Papa about French Impressionism. "He also said Monet was quite the temperamental artist."

Marcel looked at me as if I'd just told him I'd climbed the Matterhorn. "Your uncle *knew* Monet?"

"They were friends, I think. He mentioned him sometimes in his letters."

"Really?" There was a note of mischief in Marcel's voice. "I wonder if he ever mentioned *you* when he was talking to Monet."

"Don't be ridiculous!"

"It's possible, though, isn't it?"

I stood up and smoothed the skirts of my blue

silk dress before I answered him.

"Maybe," I said. "But I doubt it. Come on, I want to see the exhibit of ladies' shoes."

But Marcel reached for my hand and pulled me toward him. "Wait a minute. I've got an idea. . . . Why don't you write to Monet?"

That was the kind of harebrained scheme *I* might have come up with, but I'd never have expected it from Marcel. I couldn't tell whether he meant it or was only teasing me.

"I wouldn't dare," I said.

"Then I dare you."

If there's one thing I can't resist, it's a dare, but I wasn't about to let Marcel know that—at any rate, not just yet. "But what would I say to him?"

"Tell him how much you admire that painting, which is yours now. If he knew your uncle as well as you say he did, he's bound to reply."

"Not bad," I admitted. "*You* write the letter."

"I am not Claude MacKenzie's niece," he pointed out. "Just think, Paris—you could be starting a correspondence with one of the greatest painters in the world!"

It was a bright spring morning, about three weeks later, and I was leaning out my bedroom window, marveling at the daffodils that seemed to deck every window box along rue Cambon. Though it was barely past eight, the street was already alive with activity. Horse-drawn cabs

rattled past, an occasional auto shot through their midst, and the calls of street vendors hawking their wares rose above the traffic. It was the kind of scene my mother would have considered perfect chaos. I loved it.

"Mademoiselle!" The door to my bedroom opened, and Mme. Frenais, the housekeeper, came in. "I have been knocking," she said apologetically, "but you did not answer."

"Sorry. I guess I was so absorbed in what was going on outside"—I nodded toward the window—"that I didn't hear anything."

"There is something *inside* that ought to concern you," she said, trying to sound very stern.

"And what is that?"

With great ceremony she drew a thin envelope from the pocket of her black skirt. "This has just been delivered, mademoiselle." She handed me the letter and, smiling like Alice's Cheshire cat, left the room.

I stared after her in disbelief. It was rare for Mme. Frenais to enter my room before nine, and I'd never known her to be less than forthright. "You *must* be something special," I said aloud to the letter, and then I saw that indeed it was. The postmark was from Giverny—the village about fifty miles north of Paris where Claude Monet had made his home.

After some not-so-subtle hints from Marcel, I'd finally taken his dare and written to Monet, but it had never occurred to me that he'd actu-

ally reply. My hands were trembling as I opened the envelope. Inside was a sheet of cream-colored paper filled with a slanted, careful hand-writing. This is what it said:

Dear Mlle. MacKenzie,

I have been greatly touched by your kind-ness in writing to me. It is good to know that my work, reviled as it sometimes has been by many who style themselves professional crit-ics, is appreciated by a sensitive person such as yourself.

I may say that I do not consider you a total stranger, for I have heard your name men-tioned by your late uncle on more than one occasion. His high regard for you, mademoi-selle, was equaled by mine for him. He was a man of rare qualities and above all a loyal friend, and the news of his death has sad-dened me deeply. I extend to you my heartfelt sympathies.

What can I do for you, in return for your generous praise? Perhaps you would like to come and visit my house for a few days and give me the pleasure of showing you my gar-dens and some of my other paintings? Mme. Monet and I have plenty of room to accom-modate you and a friend, at any time that is convenient.

I await your response, and look forward to meeting you soon.

Bien vôtre,
Claude Monet

I had to read it three or four times before I could really believe it. It was like one of those stories in the penny magazines. I'd just been invited to visit one of the greatest artists in the world, and I could even bring a friend! There was no doubt in my mind who that would be— the genius who'd gotten me into this in the first place!

CHAPTER
2

Through the train window I could see miles of flat, green countryside, the same landscape I'd seen when I first arrived in France. Then it had depressed me no end, but this time, on a clear afternoon at the very end of May, everything looked positively cheerful. Maybe it was the sunlight that made such a difference, or my growing excitement as we neared Giverny, or—let's be honest—maybe it was the fact that I was traveling with Marcel.

"Are you nervous?" Marcel's voice broke into my thoughts.

"No. Why should I be?"

"I am," he admitted. "It's not every day you meet Claude Monet."

"No," I agreed, trying to envision

the fiery genius my uncle had described. "I wonder if he's really as temperamental as Uncle made him out to be." Then I remembered something. "Oh, no." I groaned.

"What is it?"

"My letter," I said. "When I wrote back to say we were coming, I didn't tell him very much about you."

Marcel looked amused. "What *should* you have told him—that I get good grades and use the proper fork when eating?"

"That's not what I mean. When I wrote back accepting his invitation, I just said that I'd be bringing a friend. Marcel, what if Monet's expecting me to bring a *girl*? Do you think he'll be shocked when I turn up with you?"

"Monet's an artist," he replied, as if that explained everything. "Why should he be shocked?"

I was about to stammer an explanation when the conductor's voice rang through the train, *"Gare Vernon. Changez pour Giverny."* Vernon Station. Change for Giverny!

The little train we caught at Vernon crawled along on its narrow-gauge track toward Giverny, twisting and turning like a caterpillar and stopping in every tiny village in that part of the Seine valley.

After cutting between the steep, thickly wooded hills around Vernon, we came out onto a bridge over the Seine itself. The broad river,

studded with green islands, gleamed and sparkled spectacularly below us. Then we were on level ground again, winding among the slopes of the northern bank.

Hawthorne and apple trees were in blossom. The fields were full of flowers. Poplar trees lined the banks of little streams.

No wonder Monet had decided to make his home here. For an artist in love with color and light, there surely couldn't be a more perfect place.

"Giverny!" a porter shouted.

Altogether about a dozen passengers got off. They all left the station with the confidence of people who knew where they were going and how to get there. Within moments Marcel and I were alone—and then someone, walking so rapidly he nearly collided with the two of us, came around the corner of the station house.

"A thousand pardons, mademoiselle," he said with a small bow.

He was what I would have called an artistic type. He wore a jacket with patched elbows, a bright purple shirt, and a green wool beret. I guessed him to be about Marcel's age, twenty-one, though he was clean-shaven, and there was something about his face that made him look more boyish.

He looked at us intently and then smiled. "Perhaps," he said, eying our luggage, "I can help you into town?"

"No, that's all right," I told him. "We're not going into town. We're staying very near here—at Monsieur Monet's house."

"Monet?" His smile faded. "He is not an easy man to visit. I fear, mademoiselle, that you may wish to stay in town after all."

"What?" Marcel sounded annoyed.

"Nothing . . ." The smile returned again. "Perhaps you will find him more charming than do the rest of us." Then, doffing his beret, he again bowed and set off toward the village.

"What was that all about?" I asked when he'd gone.

Marcel shrugged. "Maybe he had a run-in with Monet. Or maybe it's what your uncle said—we're about to visit a temperamental *artiste*."

There was no time for further speculation. A smartly dressed young man approached us, his hand already extended. He, too, was in his early twenties, though a black, squarely trimmed beard made him look older.

"It *is* Mademoiselle MacKenzie, isn't it?"

"Yes, and this is my friend, Monsieur Fleury."

He shook Marcel's hand, too, and gave a very correct bow. "I am so pleased to make your acquaintance. Allow me to welcome you to Giverny. My name is Jean-Pierre, and I am here to receive you on behalf of Monsieur Claude Monet. I have been entrusted to conduct you to our house, the Maison du Pressoir. May I help with these?"

He picked up the heaviest of our bags, and I saw Marcel give me an exasperated look. I'd brought four valises and a hatbox, which did not seem extravagant to me, but compared to Marcel's single suitcase did look a bit excessive. The three of us managed to gather up all of the luggage.

"It isn't very far," Jean-Pierre assured us. "A few hundred meters only."

From the station forecourt we turned right, onto a road fringed by tall, shady poplars that ran alongside the railway track.

"This road is called the Chemin du Roy," Jean-Pierre said. "Our property lies on either side of it." He strode on ahead, making light of the valises he was carrying. "Do you see that fence running parallel to the far side of the track?" He nodded toward green picketing, beyond which trees stood in abundance. "That marks the boundary of the water garden."

"The one that he paints?" I asked, thinking of Uncle's picture.

"The same. It is Papa Monet's finest creation. Seven years ago he had the pools dug, and now it looks as if it has always been part of the landscape."

But I was not paying attention to the history of the garden. I'd been trying to figure out just who Jean-Pierre was. "You're . . . you're his son?" I asked.

For a moment Jean-Pierre looked surprised;

then he grinned, looking slightly abashed.

"I'm so sorry I failed to introduce myself properly. I'm Jean-Pierre Hoschedé, not Papa Monet's son but his stepson. For all that, he has truly been a father to me and my brothers and sisters."

We walked along for some distance, and then Jean-Pierre halted outside a large wrought-iron gate built into a high wall. With a slight bow he said, "Welcome to the Maison du Pressoir."

Poppies, irises, peonies, and tulips that rose like islands of red and yellow from a purple sea of aubretias were just a few of the flowers I could identify among a host of others I couldn't. There was color on every side, like an immense palette of paint spread out on the earth. And the different scents of all those flowers mingled and interlaced to produce a rich, heady bouquet that fairly intoxicated me.

At the far end of the garden stood the house, a very long, two-story building, with a façade of pink and white, offset by green doors, windows, and shutters. A raised veranda ran along the front, with a green railing at its edge and green steps up to it. I could just make out a dark figure standing inside the front door at the top of the steps. Was it Monet, waiting to welcome us? My heart began to beat a little faster.

The garden was crossed by a network of straight paths. The broadest, along which Jean-Pierre now guided us, led directly from the gate

to the front door. We walked under a series of arched trellises, entwined with roses just coming into bud. I gazed up at them, enraptured.

"Mademoiselle! Please—be careful where you tread!"

Jean-Pierre's cry brought me back to reality. I looked down and saw why he'd been so alarmed. The nasturtiums that grew along both sides of the path were so rampant that in many places they'd overflowed their borders. To avoid stepping on them, one had to follow a zigzag course up the path—whereas I'd been tramping along in pretty much a straight line.

"Please excuse my shouting, mademoiselle," he apologized. "But Papa Monet would be furious if a single flower were to be damaged. And I don't like to imagine what Duran would have to say about it."

"Who's Duran?" I asked as I tiptoed gingerly around the nasturtiums.

"The head gardener. A very forthright man." Jean-Pierre lowered his voice, as if he feared Duran might be lurking among the poppies. "Personally, I would prefer the *grande allée* to be cleared of all encroachments. Not that I wish to malign the little nasturtiums, you understand, but Duran guards every blossom as if it were a national treasure. I say, every flower in its proper place. . . . Ah, *Maman*, allow me to introduce Mademoiselle MacKenzie and Monsieur Fleury."

Mme. Monet was rather stout and looked to

be in her mid-sixties; her hair, pure white, was swept back from her forehead. She had what might have been a handsome face if it hadn't looked so tired—and there was a distant expression in her cool gray eyes, as if they were fixed on something only she could see. She wore a black dress with a high neck and no frills, which struck me as rather unseasonable for a warm May afternoon.

"Good afternoon, mademoiselle." Her voice was very light and frail.

"Good afternoon, madame."

"Monsieur."

"It is an honor, madame," Marcel said, making a respectful bow.

"Jean-Pierre, please take our guests' luggage inside."

"At once, *Maman*." He darted a brief, rather nervous smile in my direction. "I look forward to seeing you both at dinner."

There was an awkward silence after he had gone. Mme. Monet did not invite us into the house. In fact, she seemed to have forgotten us altogether. She was again gazing off into the shadows of the garden. I only hoped she was expecting Monet to appear and that he would do so quickly. But no one materialized out of the shadows.

I had to say something to break the ice. As usual, it was the first thing that came into my head.

 20

"I like your garden, madame."

She sighed. "Ah . . . yes, the garden. That is my husband's domain." Suddenly she looked straight at me, frowning. "Do you know my husband?"

I was pretty surprised by that question. Surely Monet had told his wife something about me?

"Er, no—not yet," I stammered. "But I wrote him about one of his paintings, and he invited me here—me and my friend, I mean—to meet him."

"Oh . . ." Mme. Monet's gaze wandered to somewhere over the top of my head. Then she blinked and peered at my face again. "I'm sorry, what was your name?"

"Paris MacKenzie."

"Yes, of course." She raised her hand and touched her forehead with her fingertips. "Please forgive me. I have so much on my mind. Yes, we are expecting you. That was why Jean-Pierre had to go to the station, wasn't it? And my husband . . . I must apologize for his absence. As usual, he went off to work in the water garden after lunch. I believe he intended to return in time to welcome you, but he is so forgetful. When he paints, he enters another world, and neglects his duties in this one."

"That's all right," I said. "We quite understand."

There was another awkward silence. Mme. Monet didn't seem to know how to detach her-

self from us. Fortunately, I had an idea.

"As it's such a lovely day," I said, "do you think we could go off on our own for a while and have a look round the garden?"

"By all means, mademoiselle. I have to go in and help Marguerite with the dinner preparations. The garden is at your disposal—only, please take care not to tread on the flowers. And, if you wish to see the water garden, I implore you to go no farther than the bridge. My husband hates to be disturbed at his work."

She turned to go indoors, then turned back.

"Dinner at seven sharp. You will hear the bell. Please don't be late, on any account." And she disappeared inside.

· "Whew!" I said to Marcel as we walked away. "Not quite the reception I'd expected. Come on. I want to see the bridge."

We started back down the *grande allée*.

"Now, remember," Marcel said, wagging a finger at me, "you can do anything you like in this garden, so long as you don't tread on the nasturtiums."

We started to giggle at that, but shushed each other, for fear of lurking gardeners.

"Oh, isn't it heavenly!" I said. "This smell! Mmmm! Paintings are wonderful to look at, but they can't touch the real thing."

We zigzagged our way back to the wrought-iron gate.

"Straight ahead for the bridge, I guess." I

pointed to a green wooden-slatted door, on top of a rise at the other side of the railroad track.

We crossed the Chemin du Roy, passed through a gap in the line of poplars, and picked our way over the track. A short walk up the gentle bank on the other side and we were at the green door.

Suddenly I felt a thrill run through me—a delicious, expectant sensation. It was as if we were on the threshold of some secret, enchanted land, not bound by the normal laws of time and space.

I held my breath as Marcel pushed open the green wooden door. The very next thing I knew I *was* in another world, for the door led directly onto the Japanese bridge that I'd gazed at so often in Uncle's painting.

It was a simple wooden footbridge. Thick wisteria vines wound through its railing, their pink flowers trailing into the stream below.

"Oh, Marcel," I murmured as he closed the garden door and came to join me. "It's even more beautiful than I'd imagined."

With the afternoon sun on our backs, we gazed out over the widening expanse of the lily pool. Weeping willows and alders grew close by the water's edge. Their yellow-green reflections were cut through by the lily pads that floated gently on the water's surface. Dotted along the banks were clusters of blue irises, the occasional orange-red poppy, and large bushes of pale pink

azaleas and rhododendrons. The colors here were more subdued than in the flower garden, as if this place had been created to be a haven, a refuge from the world.

"It's extraordinary." Marcel's voice beside me was hushed, almost reverential. Then he smiled. "And very romantic." He bent slowly toward me, cupped his hand under my chin, and lifted my face. I knew he was going to kiss me, and my heart was beating like mad. Suddenly I felt impossibly shy. I glanced away, down toward the water.

And then I screamed.

There was a body floating facedown among the lilies.

CHAPTER
3

Marcel raced across the wooden bridge. I tried to follow him, but couldn't. I was stuck fast, clutching at the handrail, with the echo of my scream ringing over and over inside my head. At last it faded, and I staggered across the bridge to Marcel.

He'd dragged the body onto the grass bank and was kneeling beside it. As I reached him he turned it onto its back.

The man couldn't have been much over thirty. He was dressed in a coarse jacket and pants and a shirt without a collar. His hair was close-cropped, his thin face grizzled, and the skin under the mat of whiskers was the most ghastly, bloodless white I'd ever seen.

Suddenly there were voices, and with them came footsteps on the bridge—Jean-Pierre, followed by a heavy, bald man, who was puffing heavily and brandishing a trowel like a weapon.

"Mam'selle!" called Jean-Pierre. "Are you all right? Your scream—"

He broke off as he caught sight of the body. The bald man halted and crossed himself hastily. Just for a moment it must have looked to them as if Marcel were responsible for whatever had happened. Then they came forward, and I explained quickly.

"What a shock for you!" Jean-Pierre exclaimed. "Are you sure you're all right?" He sounded more concerned for me than the dead man.

"I'm all right, thanks. But what about him? Do you know who he is?"

The bald man answered. "He is Antoine Laroche, rest his soul."

"One of the carpenters Papa Monet hired last year to build a second studio," added Jean-Pierre. "He worked so well that we kept him on as a general handyman."

We were interrupted by another voice, loud and irascible, approaching from across the bridge.

"What's the meaning of this disturbance? All this noise! Jean-Pierre, Duran! Am I never to be left in peace? How can I paint when . . ."

The source of this outburst was a bulky old man in country tweeds, black leather boots, and a broad-brimmed felt hat. In one hand he held a lighted cigarette, in the other an artist's paintbrush. The most striking thing about him was a long, bushy Santa Claus beard, which would have been white but for the nicotine stains streaking it.

And that was how I first met Claude Monet, one of the greatest painters of the time: he first glared at me and Marcel, then stared at the body in puzzlement, quite visibly trying to take in what was happening in his garden.

Jean-Pierre rapidly explained to his stepfather what had been going on. Monet pulled off his hat.

"Mademoiselle MacKenzie, forgive me," said the painter gruffly. "I had no means of knowing . . . This poor fellow, though. That such a thing should happen here!"

He turned abruptly to Jean-Pierre.

"You say you heard Mademoiselle MacKenzie scream. Where were you?"

"Up at the house, Papa. I was just coming downstairs."

"Then others might have heard it?"

"Certainly. I said I'd go and find out what it was about."

"You mean, *Maman* heard it?"

Jean-Pierre nodded.

Monet looked agitated.

"Go at once," he ordered Jean-Pierre. "Give any explanation you like, except the truth. She must on no account hear of this death. You understand me?"

"Yes, Papa. But what—"

"Use your imagination, boy! Any story will do. But hurry, before she comes to find out for herself."

Jean-Pierre took to his heels and Monet turned to the gardener.

"The police will have to be informed, Duran. Go at once to the village and tell Sergeant Houlbeque in person. Not a word to another soul. Ask the sergeant, for me, to be discreet. He and his men must not come to the house. Madame must suspect nothing—*nothing*."

Duran touched his forehead with a finger and lumbered off. That left me and Marcel alone with Monet—and a corpse, which, for some reason, his wife must not be told about.

It was only now that he took my hand to raise it to his lips in proper greeting. I introduced Marcel, and Monet shook his hand.

"I ask your pardon, Mademoiselle MacKenzie, Monsieur Fleury. I had scarcely imagined welcoming you in such circumstances. . . ." Then his voice trailed off, and he was gazing at a spot on the bank a short distance from the body. "The irises," he said in a choked voice. "My God, it's starting again!"

On the far bank of the stream a bed of deep

blue irises had been planted. I imagine they had once been very beautiful. But someone had cut through them, as if with a scythe, and now not a flower remained on its stalk.

"What is starting again?" I asked.

"It is nothing, mademoiselle," Monet replied brusquely. His eyes went back to the body. "Poor Laroche. A good man. To have drowned in such shallow water. . . . It is hard to imagine such an accident."

"Or why someone would cut down a bed of flowers," I added.

Monet turned on me. "Mademoiselle," he began, "you may be Claude's niece, but you have no—"

"Monsieur Monet," Marcel broke in, "permit me to suggest that Laroche's death might not have been an accident."

Monet regarded Marcel sharply. "Not . . . how do you mean?"

Marcel knelt beside the body again and lifted one of the arms. I gasped as he pointed to a long, ragged pink gash along the wrist.

"A serious wound, monsieur," said Marcel. "And not the kind acquired by falling into a shallow stream."

"No. No, indeed. But—suicide! Impossible! Normal, healthy men like Laroche don't take their own lives."

"He may have been in some trouble," I ventured.

"No, no. He was a quiet, God-fearing fellow, to the best of my recollection. Perhaps he gashed himself at his work, became faint from the loss of blood, and collapsed into the stream."

"Perhaps." Marcel did not sound convinced.

"This is a terrible thing, a terrible thing." Monet began to pace.

"If you wish, sir," Marcel said, "we will stay with the body until the police come."

Monet's face lit with relief. "Thank you. I would like to tend to my wife. Jean-Pierre is certain to return for you at any moment. I will see you this evening at dinner."

He went off quickly, and despite the circumstances, I couldn't help smiling at Marcel. "You're getting crafty," I told him.

"I told you once before," he replied, "you're not the only Sherlock Holmes in the world."

"I know, but seriously, are you thinking what I am?"

"Probably." He walked over to the point on the bank where the irises had been cut down. "But tell me what you're thinking anyway."

Sherlock Holmes had been my personal hero for years, and now Marcel was hooked on him. It seemed natural, and even comforting, that at a moment like this we were talking in Baker Street terms. "You know my methods," I said. "Eliminate the impossible, then investigate what's left."

"Monet eliminated suicide confidently enough."

"Yes, but Laroche might not have been as sane as Monet thought. . . . Marcel, why did the irises bother him so? He seemed more upset about them than Laroche. And why was he so worried about his wife finding out about this?"

"Excellent questions," Marcel said with a grin.

"Thanks a lot. . . . Look, suppose Monet is right, that it wasn't suicide. What do you think of his accident theory?"

"I think," Marcel said, "that it's ridiculous. If Laroche really cut himself and staggered along this way, meaning to cross the bridge and go to the house for help, there would have been a trail of blood."

I looked around. There wasn't even a drop of blood near the body.

"If it was an accident," Marcel went on, "it had to have happened here. The stream's too shallow to have carried a body from another point."

"I agree," I said. "There would have been blood here if there was an accident. And there aren't any tools lying around or even a sharp rock that might have cut him."

"But someone did slice through these irises," said Marcel, examining the butchered stems, "with something very sharp—sharp enough to do a clean job . . . and perhaps to have slit Laroche's wrist."

"Maybe the knife is in the water," I suggested, at which point I took off my boots and stock-

ings, gathered up my skirts, and waded in. Marcel rolled up his trouser legs and followed. It felt deliciously cool, but we soon realized that all we were doing was stirring up the mud on the bottom. There was no knife to be found.

"Maybe it *was* an accident," I conceded, scrambling back onto the bank. "Laroche was cut somewhere else, and by the time he reached the lily pond he'd stopped bleeding. Do you think that's possible?"

Marcel hesitated before answering. "No. I don't. It's just that . . . well, if we rule out suicide, and we rule out an accident . . ."

I knew what he was reluctant to say because I was thinking the same thing.

What Sherlock Holmes had actually said was that once you'd eliminated the impossible, whatever remained, *however improbable,* must be the truth. An accident seemed physically impossible, and somehow I trusted Monet's elimination of suicide. That left the improbable: murder.

CHAPTER
4

Dinner that evening was positively maddening. Monet sat at one end of the long wooden table, his wife sat opposite him, and Marcel, Jean-Pierre, and I sat in between. Everyone was quiet as servants began to lay out an elaborate spread of roasted meats, fresh breads, condiments, and four different wines.

"You see," Jean-Pierre said with a smile, "even so far from Paris, Papa Monet has a gourmet cuisine."

Frankly, I couldn't get up much enthusiasm for the food. How could anyone eat after the events of the afternoon? Nevertheless, Monet, Jean-Pierre, and even Marcel made a brave show of it.

Mme. Monet was distracted, as she'd been when we first met her.

I suppose I was staring into space. Jean-Pierre thought I was admiring the ceramic vases across the room and immediately launched into a speech about Monet's love of Oriental art. "It was a detail in a Japanese woodblock print that gave him the inspiration for the bridge in the water garden," he said. There was a curious group reaction. Both Monet and Marcel winced, Mme. Monet glared at Marcel, and Jean-Pierre flushed. For my part, I couldn't get the image of the dead Laroche out of my mind, especially the specter of his blanched face.

"Mademoiselle MacKenzie," said Jean-Pierre hurriedly, "you must tell us how you like living in Paris."

There followed an exceptionally polite and proper conversation, masterminded by Jean-Pierre.

First, he described their large and rather complicated family. Both Monet and his wife had children from previous marriages. Now most of those children were married with families of their own. We'd come at an unusual time, he explained, when he was the only one in residence.

He then inquired as to whether we'd visited the Grand Exposition, how Marcel liked his studies, and what I thought of the Parisian fashions, and followed that with a guidebook-perfect description of the village of Giverny. This got us through appetizers and the first half of the main course. Neither Monet nor his wife had said anything and, of course, no one mentioned the irises or the fact that someone they all knew had been found dead on the grounds that very afternoon. I was beginning to wonder if Marcel and I had imagined the corpse. It was unnerving to find myself part of such a bizarre conspiracy of silence.

When Jean-Pierre eventually ran out of safe subjects, Monet himself took over. "You have noticed the light?" he asked us. "The light in this part of the country is unique. You must look carefully, Mademoiselle MacKenzie, and then you will start to notice things that you have not seen before. In Giverny it is possible to see differently."

As if deftly passing a ball between them, Jean-Pierre and Marcel joined in. Unlike Monet and Jean-Pierre, Marcel was not trying to cover anything up. He was just fascinated by Monet. And even I was getting distracted by Monet's passion for his art.

By the end of the meal only Mme. Monet had had little to say. She sat remote at her end of the table, her eyes downcast except for the odd moment when she'd look up to glare furiously at Marcel. I could see that this puzzled Marcel but, like the rest of us, he seemed bound by an unspoken agreement to make no mention of what-

ever it was that was actually going on. So everyone was surprised when Mme. Monet suddenly spoke out, addressing herself to me.

"It is a shame, mademoiselle, that your day should have been spoiled by that distressing affair in the water garden."

So she'd heard about it after all! I could feel a ripple of alarm from the others at the table.

"*Maman,* please," begged Jean-Pierre, putting his hand on her arm. "You will only upset the young lady further. What's past is past."

"Don't speak to me of the past," she retorted, drawing her arm away. "I was a girl once, and I have daughters of my own. Young girls should be warned. And you—" She turned to Marcel, her eyes flashing, and I thought, Well, at least we'll finally have it out. But Monet cut her off.

"My dear Alice," he said firmly, "you still have not told me what you thought of the 937-YZ."

I wondered what oddity I should hear next from this strange family. Mme. Monet looked equally baffled; but suddenly her frown vanished, and she smiled.

"I'm sorry. It slipped my mind. Monet, the 937-YZ is simply magnificent—everything I'd hoped it would be!"

With evident relief, Monet said, "I'm so glad."

Mme. Monet was a woman transformed. "It's so exciting!" she cried, actually turning to Marcel to include him in her enthusiasm. "A brand-new Panhard, you know. Oh, I'm so

thrilled. I can't wait to go for a drive. When may we go, Monet?"

"Very soon, my dear—now that I have hired a reliable chauffeur."

She actually clapped her hands, like a child with a new toy. Her particular new toy turned out to be a Panhard-Levassor automobile, with the registration number 937-YZ. "I do hope he can drive fast!" she said.

Monet laughed, and all of the evening's earlier tension was suddenly gone. He eagerly informed his wife of their chauffeur's qualifications, assuring her that Sylvain was a very safe, capable driver.

The car conversation had taken us through dessert, so it was on a much happier note that dinner ended, and Jean-Pierre offered to escort his mother to her room.

When they'd gone, Monet turned to us with concern. "My dear guests, I'm afraid I owe you an apology. My wife heard your scream this afternoon, and so Jean-Pierre . . . fabricated . . . a story. He told my wife that you screamed because Monsieur Fleury had been . . . too forward."

Marcel let out a sigh of relief. "So that's what it was. I couldn't imagine what I'd done to offend her."

I was not as relieved. Monet and his household were still covering up a murder, and I was fast beginning to suspect that Mme. Monet had something to do with it. How could anyone whose personality went through such rapid-fire turnabouts be completely trustworthy?

Monet frowned as he lit a cigarette. "As to that incident . . . the police have removed the body. They have found nothing suspicious, but they did ask that the two of you call at the station in the morning to make a simple statement."

"They found nothing?"

But Monet went on as if he hadn't heard me. "I know what a trying day this has been for you. You are free to retire to your rooms whenever you wish, of course. But will you first allow me to give you a brief tour of the house?"

"We'd be honored," Marcel replied smoothly, and that was the end of any mention of Laroche.

Monet led us from the cheerful yellow dining room into a much larger room whose walls were hung with paintings. "A small selection of my own work," he announced.

It was like being in a garden. Bright, vibrant colors offset by shadowy leaves and trees flowed from every surface. Now I knew what Marcel had meant when he spoke of paintings that could open a window into a world beyond reality. Around me were blossoms, poplars, haystacks, cathedrals, men and women moving in the shade of trees—all things I'd seen before, and yet it was as if I was seeing their essence for the first time, as if Monet had uncovered their

very souls with his brush strokes.

"I sell most of my work," Monet was saying. "But I've kept these paintings for reasons of sentiment. When I come in here to relax a little, they remind me of happy moments in my life."

Marcel wandered off by himself to examine some of the canvases more closely. Monet took the opportunity to say to me quietly, "I was so sorry, my dear, to hear of your uncle's death. He will be greatly missed, in the world of art as well as that of science. But nobody has been able to tell me how he died. There was some talk of a seizure, but one has also heard rumors . . . excuse me—the subject must be a painful one to you."

"Actually, I never even met my uncle," I said. "He died on the morning that I arrived in France." Then I told him about Mme. Méduse—a woman in the exclusively male world of French scientists. Unable to gain recognition on her own, Méduse approached Uncle to ask him to sponsor her. Unfortunately, what she wanted him to sponsor was her discovery of a lethal nerve gas. Uncle refused, and there'd been an angry confrontation in his study. Somehow—Méduse swore it had been an accident—a small container of the gas was broken. Méduse fled to safety, but Uncle inhaled the fumes and never regained consciousness.

"What a terrible experience for you," Monet said. "To arrive all alone in a strange land,

and to such shocking circumstances!"

I've never really known how to respond to sympathy. "Finding friends here has made it easier," I said, looking at Marcel, who was still absorbed in the paintings.

"Well, at least you've found one who appreciates art," Monet said dryly. "Come. You've seen enough of my work. Let me show you my personal collection of modern masterpieces."

To my surprise he led us into his bedroom. Every square inch of the bedroom and the washroom beyond was covered with canvases. Vast, tiny, medium-sized, they clashed in a wild, astonishing variety of styles and tones.

"My good friend Renoir did this," said Monet, pointing to a portrait of a beautiful woman reading. "Perhaps you recognize the model," he added with a smile.

I looked more closely and realized with a jolt that I *did* recognize her. It was a younger, happier Mme. Monet.

"This is Degas," Monet went on. "See how his composition derives from the Japanese technique? He's adapted it to achieve this most marvelous effect of informality. Ah, and what do you say to this, monsieur? The work of a true genius—if only he would let himself believe us when we tell him so."

"Paul Cézanne?" Marcel hesitated.

"Bravo! Doesn't that prove my point—a recognizable style—and such quality! But see here,

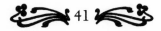

too—Renoir again, Pissarro, Sisley, Manet, who so many confuse with me—"

"But no Monet," Marcel remarked, looking around.

"Not in here, my boy. This is where I contemplate the greater works of others, and remind myself that we are all eternal students, always learning, striving."

"Do you have one favorite, Monsieur Monet?" I asked.

He shook his head. "Different works, different styles, different colors, different moods. But you, my dear—whom might you choose?"

"I don't know," I said. "They're all wonderful. I choose more time to decide."

"Fair enough," he said with a laugh. Then he turned to Marcel.

"And you, monsieur?"

"To be perfectly frank, monsieur, Vincent van Gogh."

It earned him a great slap on the back.

"Well said! Admirable not only for his vision, his boldness, his palette—but for his integrity, his moral courage. And to have died without a single work sold!"

"Didn't he cut off his ear?" I asked.

Marcel nodded. "Part of it. He had a quarrel with Gauguin, and—"

"Damn Gauguin!" roared Monet, nearly scaring me out of my wits. "He made van Gogh's final days misery. May he never return from . . ."

"Tahiti," said Marcel helpfully.

Monet turned on us, glowering. "France is well rid of Gauguin! Mademoiselle, monsieur, I am glad you have come and wish your stay here to be pleasant, but I'm afraid you must excuse me now. I rise early to paint and so must retire for the evening."

"Of course," I said, backing toward the door with definite relief. "We'll see you tomorrow."

"*Bonne nuit,* monsieur," said Marcel smoothly, as if he hadn't even noticed the outburst.

It was all I could do not to race down the hallway. "Marcel," I whispered, "we've got to talk!"

"Not in here. Let's take a walk."

The entire Monet household, servants included, seemed to retire early. There was no one around as we made our way downstairs and back into the garden. It was a perfect night, clear, crisp, and bright with stars.

"Mercy!" I said as the heady scent of the flowers hit me. "Why can't they make a perfume like this?"

By the light of a nearly full moon I could see Marcel grinning. "Is that what you wanted to talk about?"

"Actually, I thought we might discuss the masters of modern art."

"I see," he said gravely. "Anyone in particular?"

"Yes," I said, all joking over. "Claude Monet.

Claude Monet and his whole crazy household. What on earth is going on here?"

Marcel didn't answer but sat down beneath one of the tall yews that stood at the head of the *grande allée*.

"That was one of the strangest evenings I've ever spent," I said, settling down beside him. "A man is found dead on the grounds, Monet looks at some mangled flowers as if he's seeing a ghost, and four hours later everyone sits down to dinner and no one even mentions it."

"They were protecting Madame Monet."

"From what?"

"Well, you've got to admit she's not exactly stable. Distant one minute, angry the next, and like a child on Christmas morning two seconds after that."

"But no one in this house is stable! I thought Monet was going to bite our heads off when you mentioned Gauguin. And right after he'd been playing the charming host. As for Jean-Pierre, he distracts his mother from the truth, us from his mother . . . I think they're all crazy. Marcel, what if Madame Monet had something to do with the death and they're all covering for her?"

"I like Monet," he said, ignoring my question. "Besides, he was your uncle's friend. That ought to count for something." Marcel reached out into the darkness. "Cup your palm," he instructed. I did and he gently set a firefly inside.

"None of this changes the fact that he didn't

seem very concerned about Laroche's death," I pointed out. The firefly walked onto the top of my hand, then flew into the night, winking.

"Artists are different," Marcel said with a shrug. "Just look at Monet's paintings. You can see that he's tied more closely to nature than to the human form."

"Don't *you* start making excuses," I said. I got up. "I'm going to find out how Antoine Laroche died. And then I'm going to find out why everyone in this house is pretending it never happened. Are you with me or not?"

Suddenly Marcel was standing, gripping me tightly by the arms. "How can you even ask that?" he demanded.

I saw his point; in the short time I'd known him, Marcel had risked his life for me more times than I could count. "I'm sorry," I said. "That wasn't fair."

"No," he said more gently, "it wasn't." His voice softened. "Paris, you ought to know by now—for as long as you want, I'll be with you."

I looked into his eyes and knew he was telling the truth.

CHAPTER
5

I couldn't get to sleep that night. The little guest room I'd been given was comfy enough, and I was certainly tired, but long after I'd extinguished the bedside oil lamp, I lay awake, my mind whirling. The face of Antoine Laroche, pale and mournful as the moon, kept rising before me. How could I lay the poor soul's ghost to rest? Only by doing what I'd vowed to do—by finding out how and why he died.

When I finally realized this, I gave up all hope of sleep. I got out of bed, slipped on a dressing gown, and began pacing the room.

Before long I was deep in an imaginary conversation with my old friend Dr. Watson. "First, we

must review the possibilities," I said. "We've ruled out accident, so it had to be suicide or murder."

"But which?" asked Watson.

"If the man had decided to kill himself," I answered, "why choose to do it in Monet's water garden? Out of spite? Unlikely. Anyway, Monet spoke kindly of the man. He seemed to like him. So far, we have no reason to suspect that the affection wasn't mutual."

"Indeed, Holmes," Watson agreed, "suicide seems highly unlikely."

Drat! Was I really getting mixed up in another murder case?

For the first time I considered the police. Surely if they suspected murder, they would have been all over the grounds. And they would have questioned the witnesses—Marcel and me.

But they hadn't. Did they believe Laroche's death had truly been an accident? Were they prepared to accept the simplest explanation because no weapon had been found? I knew they wouldn't stay away simply because Monet had asked them to. No artist had *that* kind of influence.

And how did the irises fit in? I couldn't forget that Monet seemed far more distressed over them than over the death. The two were certainly connected—but the piece that connected them was missing. "Watson" and I supplied about a dozen possible explanations, but none

of them actually made sense.

What would Holmes do? I wondered. The answer was simple: he would return to the scene of the crime and make sure that no clue had been overlooked. I couldn't face the idea of bothering to put on a dress, but I did pull on stockings and shoes and made sure that my dressing gown was fastened.

Though my boots sounded terribly loud on the plain wooden floorboards, I made it safely across the landing and downstairs. I'd half expected the front door to be locked, but it wasn't. Apparently they didn't worry about thieves here in the country.

I stepped out onto the porch and closed the door quietly behind me. Then I set off toward the bridge and garden. It must have been about an hour before dawn, because the sky had already begun to lighten. In the gray light the garden looked completely different than it had during the day—drained of all color, almost as if it had snow on it.

When I reached the gate, which was unlocked, I looked to the left and right. I was alone, and the garden was absolutely silent. I crossed the railroad track, walked up the little rise, put out my hand to open the slatted wooden door to the bridge—and froze. There was someone standing on the bridge.

Maybe a more prudent person would have taken the cue to skedaddle. Not yours truly. I just had to know who was on the other side of that door.

Moving as quietly as I could, I peered through the wooden slats. I saw a woman wearing a dark shawl on her head. Her face was turned away from me, and I felt a chill run up my spine as I realized that she was staring at the very place in the stream where we'd found the body of Antoine Laroche.

At length she turned and began to walk toward me. It was Mme. Alice Monet.

In pure desperation, I managed to hide myself behind a very large, dew-covered peony bush. Any normal person would have heard me scuffling around; despite my love of detective stories, I'm not very good at trailing people. But Mme. Monet walked as if she were in a trance. She left the bridge, closed the gate behind her, crossed the tracks, and started toward the house without even glancing in my direction.

The sun had just risen by the time I deemed it safe to return. I'd just reached the *grande allée* when it occurred to me that the servants might be awake now, and I didn't want to have to explain sneaking *into* the house. I couldn't just walk up the main path, and I wasn't about to risk cutting through the flower beds. It took some doing, but finally I found my way back by going through the fields that bordered the garden. My boots had begun to make a horrible squishing sound, and my dressing gown and

nightgown were plastered to my legs. To say that I was happy when at last I reached the house is an understatement.

Then I heard voices coming from the open kitchen window.

"I have nothing against them," said Mme. Monet, her voice wavering as if she were about to cry. "It's only that this is not a good time for visitors."

"As good as any other and better than some." Monet sounded weary.

"Nevertheless, I would like you to ask them to leave. They can stay the day and depart tomorrow morning."

"My dear Alice." Monet was obviously straining not to shout. "This household must and *will* return to normal. That girl is the niece of a man who was my friend. I will not ask her to leave. Besides, you will see, it will be good for you. With so many of the children away . . . oh, damn!"

Alice had broken into tears and was sobbing as if she'd never stop.

I was beginning to feel very embarrassed. This was a conversation I was clearly never meant to hear. So I set off around the house until I found a back door. Luck was with me again. It, too, had been left open, and I was able to return to my room undetected.

Too tired to make sense of what I'd just heard, I stripped off my wet boots and clothes and fell

 50

onto the bed. I don't even remember pulling the
covers up—that's how quickly I fell asleep.

CHAPTER
6

Shortly after nine that morning Marcel and I were on our way into Giverny to talk to the police. Though I was feeling very foggy, having had only three hours' sleep, I took it as a good sign that I'd been awakened for breakfast; obviously no one suspected that I'd been out at dawn.

I had filled Marcel in on what I'd seen and overheard as we walked. "Well, it's interesting," he said, "but it doesn't really tell us any more about Laroche's death."

"You don't think it casts definite suspicion on Madame Monet?"

"Why? Because she wants us to leave?"

"No." We'd turned off a narrow

street called rue des Chandeliers; the police station was just up ahead. "Because of where I saw her. Haven't you ever heard of the murderer returning to the scene of the crime?"

"Of course, but—"

"I think she's connected to the death," I went on. "First we have her returning to the scene of the crime, then she tells her husband she doesn't want us here. Obviously, she's afraid we suspect something."

"Well, if she's guilty and Monet's covering for her, then why would he insist that we stay?"

"Because it's the best cover they could possibly have," I replied. "The appearance that everything is normal."

Marcel looked at me with concern. "You may be right, Paris, but we can't go around making charges like that until we have more solid evidence."

"I know," I said more to myself than to him, "and I'm going to get it."

Sergeant Houlbeque, portly and cheerful looking, beamed at us across the station counter.

"Mademoiselle, *and* monsieur, it's so gracious of you to come forward promptly in response to my request. If only all our citizens were as public-spirited as you, our job would be much easier. Isn't that a fact, Henri?"

"It is indeed, sir." The tall young gendarme standing behind the sergeant made a slight but very correct bow as he spoke.

"We shall be pleased to help, in any way possible," Marcel said.

"As it happens, monsieur, your help is exactly what we require. Is it true that monsieur is employed at the Institute for Chemical Research in Paris?"

"Yes." Marcel looked astonished. The sergeant grinned triumphantly.

"Word travels, monsieur. One has it also that mademoiselle is from America. The information, of course, came from Monsieur Jean-Pierre Monet, during our visit yesterday. A bad business. Sad. I gather that you were the finders of the body?"

Marcel told him briefly of the circumstances, which Henri noted down while the sergeant rubbed his hands and nodded.

"That is as reported," he said. "Monsieur Fleury, would you be good enough to assist us— in your professional capacity, that is?"

"How?"

"The fact is, the doctor who examined the deceased noticed traces of some chemical substance on the clothing, which he could not identify. It would mean sending the clothing away to the laboratories, which seems unnecessary in a matter where no suspicion arises. Since you were expected to call in today, it occurred to me . . ."

"I'll do my best," Marcel offered.

"Splendid. Just to tie up the last loose end,

you understand. If monsieur would kindly step this way?"

"Can't I come too?"

"It's not a sight for a young lady, mademoiselle," said Houlbeque.

"I won't be long, Paris," Marcel told me. "Why not take a look around the village? I'll find you easily, I'm sure."

He went off with the sergeant, and I lingered for a word with Henri, the gendarme.

"Monsieur Laroche's death must have been a shock—for his family, I mean."

Henri, who was shuffling through stacks of forms, didn't even look up. "He had no family," he replied. "No brothers or sisters, never married, and both parents dead."

"Then he had only the Monets."

This got me the gendarme's full attention. "You do not understand, mademoiselle. The Monets were employers, not family. They got on well enough—Antoine was a good carpenter— but he was always a little greedy."

Sure that Henri would tell me to stop being so nosy, I asked the next question anyway. "How do you mean?"

Henri was focused on his papers again. "Oh . . . it was just his personality. Pleasant, actually quite loyal to the Monets, but always wanting more. Perhaps that's why Madame Monet let him go."

"She fired him?"

"Mmmmm . . ." Henri was now sorting his forms into piles. "On the morning he died, Alice Monet let him go, and no one knows why. Furthermore, mademoiselle, no one *will* know until Monet tells her of the death and allows us to ask some questions. These artists . . ."

"Then you suspect murder too!"

I must have sounded overeager because Henri looked up at me in alarm. "We consider all possibilities, mademoiselle. I am sorry, but I am not at liberty to disclose anything more. You understand."

"Of course."

I wondered if I could slip in one more question and decided it was worth a try. "I'm sure Monsieur Laroche will be missed," I said, "after living with the Monets all these years."

Henri had taken out yet another batch of forms, having efficiently disposed of the last, and was sorting mechanically. Without breaking his rhythm he answered, "You are still making him sound like a member of the family. He did not live at the *Maison*. Like all the workers, he had a room on the grounds, but Antoine was his own man. He had his own house here in the village, number thirteen, rue des Chandeliers."

This was far more than I'd hoped to get and I half suspected Henri said it just to get rid of me. I wasted no time.

"Thank you, monsieur. I appreciate your help."

 56

"And yours, mademoiselle. Thank you for stopping by. There is just one more thing. . . ." At this he fumbled as if suddenly embarrassed. "The hotel across the way, it has quite a reputation. You know . . . the saloon. Mademoiselle would not think of entering alone. That would be quite improper."

"Oh, quite," I agreed, and left the station.

CHAPTER
7

The hotel was directly across the square from the police station. Just in case Henri was watching, I deliberately walked away from it and instead headed for the address that really intrigued me—N° 13, rue des Chandeliers.

In the midst of a row of small, well-tended houses, N° 13 was positively decrepit. Its wooden sides, which had once been white, were darkened with years of dirt, and the windows were filthy. Except for the ones that were broken, it must have been impossible to see through them. Not that anyone was likely to try; the drapes were drawn shut.

It struck me as very odd that a

house belonging to a carpenter should be in such disrepair. I was staring at it, trying to devise some logical explanation and wishing I could see inside, when a young man, wearing dark blue pants and a green velvet jacket, hurried toward the house. He stopped suddenly, smiled, and then rushed toward me. "Mademoiselle," he exclaimed, "it is so good to see you again!"

To be honest, I didn't recognize him.

"We met at the train station," he said, as if sensing my confusion. And then with a sweeping bow, "Louis Devereaux, at your service."

"Well, thank you," I said, a bit taken aback. "I'm Paris MacKenzie."

"I knew that we would meet again. And here you are in front of the very house where I am staying."

"You live here?"

"For a while. It is not luxury, but . . ." He shrugged. Then, with an engaging smile, he said, "I have been painting near the railroad station and foolishly forgot my ocher pigment. After I fetch it from my house, I wonder . . ." He paused, and I could not help but notice what a startling shade of blue his eyes were—nearly turquoise.

"You wondered?"

"If perhaps you might like to come back to my easel with me and see my painting."

If I were not so wild about Marcel, I thought, this man would have my heart in a minute. There was something exciting and very intense

about him—what my Chicago friends and I called "dash." The way he was looking at me now made me feel as if I were the only girl in France.

"Delighted," I murmured.

His eyes lit up. Then he disappeared into the house.

When he emerged with his paint, we walked to the bottom of the road, turning right into the Chemin du Roy. There, just across from the railroad station, stood his easel.

"Tell me what you think," he said. "And you must be honest."

The painting was of the old station building, and though it seemed an obvious imitation of Monet's style, there was something jaunty and cheerful about it. If he were not trying to be Monet, I thought, he'd probably be quite good.

"Well?"

"I like it."

"But? I can hear the reservation in your voice."

Once again I was about to say something better left unsaid. "But I think it's suffering from a heavy dose of Monet."

He looked at me strangely. Now I've done it, I thought. I've offended him.

"Every artist in Giverny suffers from the influence of Monet," said Devereaux finally. "He is incomparable. It is to him that each of us owes his presence here—all of us attracted to his greatness, like moths to a flame."

"Have you met him?"

"Briefly. You are staying with him, no? You can see then that he keeps to himself. Still, he is a great teacher." At this Devereaux began laughing. "He teaches that vital lesson in how to handle fame and wealth should they ever come our way. I have absorbed his lessons entirely and wait only for the chance to put them into practice." He shook his head, still laughing at himself, and began to add the ocher paint to the palette. "First, though, comes the art itself. Do you not agree?"

Actually, I didn't know what to say to any of that, and didn't much care. I was trying to figure out how I was going to ask him about Antoine Laroche. If Devereaux was living in Laroche's house, he might know something.

"And how do you like *chez Monet*?" he asked suddenly.

"The gardens are beautiful—"

"Ah, but the things that go on there . . ." He looked at me searchingly. "I'm sorry, mademoiselle. Obviously you haven't heard."

"About Laroche?"

"Then you were told."

"Told? I found his body."

At that he looked genuinely shocked. "I am sorry! What a horrible thing for you to witness. And on your first day in Giverny. . . ."

"Did you know him?" I asked. "Laroche?"

"Of course. My rooms are rented from him.

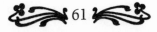

. . . I wonder if I will be thrown out. . . . You see, I had been renting a studio from Madame Baudy, at the hotel, but she decided to double the rate, and I had to find something humbler. There isn't much in Giverny that's humbler than Antoine's place, and since he spent most of his time at the Maison du Pressoir, he was willing to rent me the downstairs. I always thought he was a good man, though I never saw much of him."

"Do you think he committed suicide?"

Devereaux gave a short laugh. "He did not bare the secrets of his soul to me, but from what I know of Laroche, no. Do cats commit suicide? He was content being what he was."

"Then," I said, "it's possible that he was murdered."

Devereaux looked at me as if I'd just awakened. "It is possible."

"Do you have any idea who might have done it?"

"No, but then I am not privy to the secrets of Giverny. I am an artist."

"I don't follow you. What has one to do with the other?"

"The villagers don't like artists," he explained. "To them we are outsiders who have changed their precious village. Most of them refuse to talk to me, and they certainly won't talk to your host. I assure you, if anyone in Giverny has any information about Antoine's death, Monsieur Monet and I will be two of the last people to

find out, and then only in the newspapers."

"You don't have any suspicions of your own?"

"Mademoise—Paris, may I call you by your name?"

I nodded impatiently.

"Paris, I spend my days as you see me now— painting. What goes on among the villagers is not my concern, though of course I was sorry to hear about Antoine."

I decided to try one last question. "Have you heard anything about flowers being cut?"

Devereaux regarded me with amusement. "I will be happy to cut flowers for you . . . a bouquet of lilies, perhaps? They grow wild by the river."

"I'm sorry to have bothered you," I said, put out by his flippancy. "I'll let you return to your painting." I turned back to the town.

"Paris," he said quickly. "I—I would like to gather those flowers for you. And I would like to paint your portrait."

"My portrait?"

"You are very beautiful, you know. Will you sit for me?"

"I—I'm not sure," I said, quite surprised. "I've never modeled for anyone. And I'm not very good at sitting still."

Devereaux's voice was persuasive. "It is not as difficult as you think. We can begin with a short session—just an hour or so. Tomorrow I shall be at the house all day, working in detail on this

sketch. Why not come by about two thirty?"

Why not, indeed? Ever since I'd first seen Laroche's house, I'd wanted to get inside. Call it a hunch if you will, but I had the definite feeling that somewhere in Antoine's house was a clue to his death. Modeling was the perfect way in. On the other hand, the idea of modeling for a man I'd just met, especially a charmer like Devereaux, was . . . well, nerve-racking. I'd seen one real model at work. She'd been sitting for Stéphane, Marcel's roommate, and she was wearing a sheet. *Just* a sheet, and not a very large one at that. Was it the sort of thing that a well-bred young lady would do? It most certainly was not.

"At least try it," Devereaux persisted. "If you don't like modeling, you can just say so, and we'll stop. Say you'll come and I'll even clean the place up."

"No, no . . . that's not necessary. It's just that—"

And then I made the mistake of looking into those eyes, and all I saw was the challenge in them, laughing at me.

"All right," I said. "I'll be there at two thirty. Tomorrow."

CHAPTER
8

I stood there, quite unable to believe what I'd just agreed to do.

"Don't be nervous," said Devereaux. "I shall be very entertaining as you sit there, and before you know it, you'll have a glowing portrait."

"Of what?" asked a familiar voice. Marcel had come up behind us.

"Of me," I answered. "Marcel, this is Louis Devereaux. He's asked me to model for him."

"And will you?" asked Marcel.

"She has very graciously agreed," answered Devereaux.

"Then you have a fine subject to paint," replied Marcel. "Would you mind very much if I borrowed her

for a few minutes?"

"Not at all." Devereaux bowed. "I must return to my painting anyway."

"Don't *I* have anything to say about whether I'm 'borrowed'?" I demanded as Marcel steered me back toward the village.

He stopped, let go of my arm, and laughed. "Yes, I'm sure you do. I'm sorry, Paris. But there are things I must discuss with you, and I didn't want to stand there making polite conversation with that painter. Will you come with me to the hotel? I understand from the gendarmes that the proprietress of the hotel is something of an expert on what goes on in Giverny. She also knows the Monets quite well."

It was very hard to stay angry at Marcel. "I don't know," I told him, suppressing a smile. "Henri, the gendarme, warned me that it is not a proper place for a young lady."

"And when have you let that stop you—"

We both stepped aside as a grizzled old man, wearing a striped shirt and excessively baggy pants, drove a large cow through the center of the street. He'd almost passed us when he stopped, fixed us with a hard stare, and then said something in a rapid, heavily accented French. Although I'm nearly fluent, I could only make out two words of this: *Pressoir* and *Monet*. Then he clamped a clay pipe firmly between his jaws and moved the cow on. Marcel had turned a furious shade of red.

"What did he say?"

"He identified us as the ones from Paris staying at the Maison du Pressoir. The rest was about Monet. He called him a filthy old blundering jackass whose . . . never mind. It's not repeatable."

"Tell me!"

"Don't you want to hear what I found when I examined the body?"

"Please tell me what that man said, Marcel. I hate it when people hide things from me! It makes me feel like I'm ten again. And I assure you, I've heard bad language before."

"Then you don't have to hear it from me," Marcel replied calmly. "Take my word for it, there was nothing in what that man said that could help us. It was only a stream of invective against Monet."

"All right." I tried to sound as reasonable as he did. "Exactly what did you find on the body?"

"The jacket had traces of oil paint on it, and some chemical that photographers use for developing plates."

I was impressed. "You could tell that even though his things had been soaked in water?"

"Water doesn't wash oil away. The chemical traces were fainter, but they were there, all the same. The other thing I found was splinters—tiny ones, caught in the weave of his jacket."

"Splinters?"

"Wood. All down his back. As if he'd been

lying on a floor covered with shavings, or maybe on a woodpile. Then again, he was a carpenter. He worked with wood."

"What did the police make of that?"

"Not much. Sergeant Houlbeque's response to it was 'interesting, Monsieur Fleury. Very interesting.' Actually, there was something he was saying to Henri as I left. I didn't catch all of it, but it sounded like '. . . saboteur's back.'"

"Saboteur?"

"That's what it sounded like."

"Don't you think murder is a rather extreme form of sabotage?"

Marcel ran a hand through his hair. "No. I think they're two separate acts, possibly committed by two different people. There was Antoine's death—that's the murder. And there was the flower bed—that's the sabotage."

"But they're connected," I told him. "I don't know how, but I'm sure of it."

"Yes, Holmes," he said. "I think you're right."

"Did the police say anything about Laroche's house, whether they had searched it?"

Marcel didn't even know Antoine had a house, so I filled him in on all Devereaux had said, and this, of course, brought us back around to the subject of my modeling.

"I'm not so sure it's a good idea," Marcel said.

"How else are we going to get inside? We could sneak in—"

"Oh, no," he groaned. "Don't start that again."

68

The last time I'd proposed sneaking in somewhere, Marcel had gotten knocked over the head
and I wound up unconscious from nerve gas.*

"Then the only way in is for me to model," I
said firmly.

Marcel shook his head. "I will come with you."

"That's ridiculous. It would seem as if I didn't
trust Devereaux."

"*I* don't," he said.

"You're jealous," I replied, and instantly felt
mean for having said it.

Marcel reached out and brushed back a strand
of hair that had escaped my hairpins. "Maybe,"
he admitted. "And maybe I just trust your
hunches—if you're right, and there is some clue
in the house, then someone may try to stop you
from finding it."

"There's one more thing," I said, not willing
to be scared off. "Henri told me that Antoine
tended to be greedy, and that Madame Monet
had fired him on the morning of his death. Only
no one knows why, because Monet won't let
anyone question her."

"You still think she's responsible?" Marcel
sounded skeptical. "Personally, I think she's very
strange, but she doesn't strike me as a murder-
ess."

"I don't know," I said. "The only thing that's
clear is that she knows something no one else

* In *Mystery of the Magician*

does and Monet is covering for her."

"Time to get more information," said Marcel, nodding at the hotel. It was a cheerful-looking place with a white awning shadowing the entrance to a small courtyard. We passed a few unoccupied tables, shaded by parasols, and went in.

The notorious hotel had a very quiet entrance—a small, red-carpeted foyer with a reception counter at which a young girl sat. She looked at us without interest. There was no sign of the saloon bar. It was probably in back somewhere. I left the next move to Marcel.

He told the girl that we should like a word with the proprietor. She answered that M. Baudy was out of town, pursuing his other occupation, selling sewing machines. His wife, Mme. Baudy, was in the shop. She pointed to a connecting door.

I had noticed a shop adjoining the hotel, but hadn't realized it was part of the premises. It proved to be quite spacious, stocked from floor to ceiling with all sorts of things—domestic implements, hardware, stationery, newspapers, tobacco, bottles of wines and spirits, and even picture frames, canvases, and other artist's materials. I couldn't imagine Monet descending from his heights to shop here for a tube of paint, but no doubt the other Giverny artists did.

Mme. Baudy, thin and elderly, with pure white hair drawn back into a bun, was behind a counter, writing in a ledger. As we approached she looked up suddenly, for all the world like a startled chipmunk. She made darting little movements like a chipmunk's too.

"But of course!" she exclaimed when Marcel introduced us. "From Monsieur Monet's. Yes, yes, I heard. They have been looking forward to your visit. A pity about yesterday, but . . ." She made a little gesture of helplessness. "You've been visiting our police station, then?" Of course, she'd seen us across the way.

I took over the conversation from Marcel. "Madame. You know about the tragedy—Monsieur Laroche?"

"Nothing remains a secret long in Giverny," she said.

"Yes," said Marcel. "We noticed that."

"As a matter of fact," I said, "we noticed it this morning when we ran into an old man with a cow who seemed to know quite a bit about us." I told her what he'd said and how he'd cursed Monet.

Mme. Baudy became visibly upset. "That should never have happened."

"It doesn't matter much," I said. "No harm came of it, but why was he so angry at Monet?"

"Monet is not liked," she explained. "Over the years my husband and I have become friendly with him and his family, but the villagers will never accept him. They blame him for all the artists who have moved here . . . and just about

anything else that goes wrong. It's not his fault. They don't understand artists."

"Neither do I," I admitted, "but this man . . . it seemed like more than misunderstanding."

"He hated Monet," Marcel stated.

Mme. Baudy stared down through her glass counter at an array of penny candies. I had the sinking feeling that we were making her very uncomfortable.

"Madame," Marcel said, "did you know that there was something else that happened in the water garden, besides Laroche's death?"

"Tell me," she said.

"A bed of irises was cut down."

She looked up sharply; her face had gone quite pale. "It is happening again," she said quietly.

Marcel's voice echoed mine. "That's exactly what Monet said."

"Didn't he tell you anything else?" asked Mme. Baudy.

"No," I answered. "He's said almost nothing about the murder. Mostly he talks about painting."

"That's Monet for you." She regarded us carefully and then said, "Since you are staying at the *Maison,* I think you have a right to know what is going on—or what *has* gone on.

"Though he never intended it, Monet's coming to Giverny changed the very nature of the village. Not long after he settled here, artists, not only from France but from all over Europe

and even America, also came, as if just coming to Giverny would turn them into great painters. Well, it's been good fortune for our hotel—since Monet has been here I have never lacked customers—but most of the people in Giverny are farmers who live exactly as their fathers and grandfathers and great-grandfathers did. You can understand that they would not like this sudden invasion.

"About ten years ago the people of Giverny decided to drive Monet out. They unmoored a boat he used to paint from, they destroyed one of the haystacks he painted, and they even tried to cut down the row of poplars he was working from. Nothing terrible, you understand. Little acts."

"Harassment," Marcel said. "Like cutting down the irises."

"Yes. To his credit, Monet did not scare easily. Eventually the villagers left him alone. There has been no trouble for years."

"Then why now?" I asked.

"Now Monet wants to expand his water garden. There are farmers downstream from him who claim that the *nymphéas*, the water lilies, are poisoning the water and their cattle. Of course, this is not true. The police had the water tested, and . . ."

"The water was fine," Marcel finished.

She nodded. "Unfortunately, that did not convince everyone. The people here are not bad,

but they don't take to outsiders."

"No wonder Monet keeps to himself," I said. "Then again, he'd probably do that no matter where he was."

"You two must be very careful," she told us. "The farmers are excitable. If the sabotage has started again you might be in danger."

At that point a customer walked in. Mme. Baudy smiled as if we'd been exchanging pleasantries, and asked whether we'd seen her famous saloon.

"Well, then, I will show you," she said. She raised the counter flap and bustled through to lead us back into the foyer and toward a back room.

One glance told me that the bar was certainly not a place I should have visited alone. And by proper standards it was not a place for me to have gone at all, which meant, of course, that I loved it. There were no other women there except for the barmaid, who was pouring a drink. A billiard table took up most of the room, and though it was only midmorning, the lights were on and there were men sitting around with cues, waiting for their turn to play. The smell of tobacco was overwhelming.

"I've never been in a place like this!" I said. "Let's get a table."

Marcel shot me a look of disbelief but didn't argue.

"Now, we've got to figure out our next move,"

I said as we settled into one of the darker cor-
ners.

"Would you like something from the bar?"
Marcel asked, grinning at me. "Perhaps some
cailloutin? It's the local wine, reputed to be very
rough and strong but a must for visitors."

He knew I still hadn't gotten used to the
French custom of drinking wine with every meal
and for nearly any excuse in between.

"It's not even eleven o'clock," I protested. "I'll
have a tonic water, thank you."

He bowed, laughing. "Right away, mademoiselle."

As Marcel headed for the bar I took stock of
the patrons. There were a couple of men in the
traditional indigo-blue work smocks, obviously
locals. They were all gathered at one end of the
bar, talking quietly. With the exception of the
barmaid, no one approached them. It occurred
to me that even in a place as public as a saloon,
they kept entirely to themselves. But for the
most part the room was filled with more urbane
types. American accents mingled with British
and a few heated conversations in French. I
made a mental note to introduce myself to some
of the Americans; it always felt good to talk with
someone from home.

There were two real standouts at the bar. The
first was a gigantic bearded American in a top hat
and suit, brandishing an elegant silver-headed
walking cane. Impressive as he was, he was

clearly outdone by his companion, who wore a tartan cap and kilt and had an honest-to-goodness set of bagpipes slung over one shoulder.

"Ah, I see you are intrigued by Messieurs Dice and Metcalf," said Marcel as he returned with our drinks.

"How do you know who they are?"

"The barmaid. Together, she and Jean-Pierre could write an encyclopedia on this place. Metcalf is the big American. Apparently, when he first arrived, he spoke almost no French. He stood on Madame Baudy's doorstep, trying desperately to make himself understood; and she was so alarmed at the sight of this foreign giant that she slammed the door in his face."

"Madame Baudy? I can't believe it!"

"That was at the very beginning of the 'invasion.' Anyway, he returned a few weeks later with his easel, and she saw that he was just another painter like Monet. She got over her fears, and he turned out to be one of Giverny's most renowned artists."

"What else did you find out?"

"Not much." Marcel took a sip of his *cailloutin* and made a face. "Every bit as bad as they say. . . . I asked about your friend Devereaux. I said I'd heard he was quite good."

"And?"

"Marie—that is the barmaid—said, 'Good for everything except paying rent.' According to her, Madame Baudy always had trouble getting him to pay it."

"So?" I was surprised to find myself coming to Devereaux's defense. "Maybe he didn't want to admit to me that he hadn't the money to pay."

Marcel raised one eyebrow but said nothing.

"We've got to be back at the *Maison* soon," I said. "Lunch at twelve sharp. So, where do we stand? Let's assume that the sabotage of the irises is somehow connected with Antoine's death. That must have been what Sergeant Houlbeque meant when you overheard him talking with Henri."

"Perhaps," said Marcel, "Antoine caught the saboteur in the act and tried to stop him."

"After Madame Monet fired him? That's loyalty above and beyond the call of duty. And that brings us back to the mysterious Madame Monet. Marcel, I think we should watch her."

He frowned. "Spy on the woman who's invited us into her home?"

"Monet invited us," I pointed out.

"That doesn't matter. It's still gauche."

"Please, Marcel. If we can only find out what she knows about Antoine, we may be able to solve this."

Marcel considered his unfinished drink for a long moment. "All right, Paris, but only because I trust your 'unique' instincts."

"Then we'll stay with them for the rest of the day, and tonight we'll take turns keeping watch on the house just in case she goes for another

late-night stroll."

"I'd better take first watch," Marcel said. "You need to catch up on your sleep. I can tell."

"And," I continued, "we will make discreet inquiries in the village and try to locate this saboteur. To start with, we can find out who that old man who cursed Monet is."

"Anything else?"

"Only that tomorrow I shall uncover what I can in Antoine's house." Marcel rolled his eyes and probably would have tried to dissuade me again had not a young boy come up to the table at that moment.

Before I could wonder what he was doing in a saloon, he'd begun interrogating me. "You're staying with Monet?"

"Yes, but—"

"And you?" he demanded of Marcel.

"*Mais oui,*" answered Marcel with considerable amusement.

"Then you must take this to him."

With that he thrust a loosely folded sheet of paper into my hand and ran from the room.

The note was addressed to Monet. It read:

M. Monet,
Be warned. *You* remove the *nymphéas* or we will. Let the death of Laroche be proof—no one, least of all your guests, stops us.

"Very direct," I said. "And in line with your

 78

idea about Antoine surprising the saboteur."

"I'm going to find out who that boy is," Marcel said, already striding toward the bar.

He came back a few minutes later and reported, "No luck. Marie didn't see him, the locals aren't interested, and the English and Americans think all village children look alike."

I folded the note and slipped it into my purse. "This was written to scare us," I said.

Marcel nodded. "Whoever wrote it is serious."

"Well, that may be," I said, feeling far less brave than I sounded. "But until I find out how Antoine died, I won't stop. Let's go back to the house. This time we'll get some answers from the Monets."

CHAPTER
9

Marcel and I got back to the house at the stroke of noon. Although two rings of the bell told us we'd made it in the nick of time for lunch, Monet and his family were already seated at a table on the veranda when we arrived. Obviously, they were waiting for us, and knowing that the household kept to a very strict schedule, I expected Monet to be irritated.

"I'm sorry we're late," I began. Actually, I was furious with myself for not arriving earlier. I'd been counting on getting Monet alone and showing him the letter.

"No matter," said Monet, who sat at the head of the table looking out on the *grande allée*. He seemed to

be in a fine mood. "We often have lunch out here," he said. "When the weather's good, I love to sit and watch the sunlight moving across the flowers."

I saw that we were in for another round of "Let's pretend nothing's happened." As before, no one mentioned the death or even the irises: Monet elaborated on the hue of a particular bed of forget-me-nots, Marcel and Jean-Pierre chatted away as if they'd been lifelong friends, and Mme. Monet actually seemed cheerful. I made the necessary polite remarks and spent the rest of lunch silently reviewing the information we'd gathered.

I missed most of the conversation until Monet addressed his wife. "Well, my dear Alice, would you like to tell our guests the good news?"

"Oh, yes," she said. Then she turned to me. "You can't imagine how thrilled I am. We're going to take an excursion in the 937-YZ this very afternoon. To the automobile races at Gaillon!"

I guessed that Monet had devised this outing as a special treat for his wife. "I hope you have an enjoyable time, madame," I said.

At that, she laughed. It was the first time I'd seen her laugh, and the years seemed to fall away from her as she did so. In that moment I caught a glimpse of the beautiful woman Mme. Monet must have been, the woman Renoir had painted.

"My dear child," she said. "You don't understand. When I said *we* are going to Gaillon, I

didn't mean only Monet and myself. We're inviting you and Monsieur Fleury to come with us! Please say you will—we *shall* enjoy your company."

I glanced at Marcel and grinned. At least we'd have no trouble keeping an eye on her. "We'd love to."

"Perfect! I have scarves and goggles for you both." The transformed Mme. Monet then called to a servant and made arrangements for our riding gear. As we finished eating, Monet excused himself to change into his own "auto apparel," as he called it, and twenty minutes later we were all on the road, bound for Gaillon. There was no chance to bring up either the letter or Antoine Laroche.

I had the privilege of riding in the 937-YZ, along with Monet, his wife, and the chauffeur, Sylvain. Behind us was a Hotchkiss which belonged to Jean-Pierre, driven by him, with Marcel as his passenger.

Sleek and gleaming, the black Panhard-Levassor was a thoroughbred among automobiles. As for Sylvain, in gloves that reached to his elbows and a peaked cap pulled tightly down to shade his eyes, he was a masterly chauffeur. Sitting upright at the wheel, like a general on horseback surveying a battlefield, he drove in silence, only now and then nodding in response to Mme. Monet's exclamations of delight.

I sat in the back next to Monet. He didn't talk

much, mainly because he didn't have to. His wife chattered all the way, pointing out landmarks and exclaiming with excitement whenever the car lurched unexpectedly—which was quite often, despite Sylvain's skill, because the roads were so rough and rutted. It was a far cry from the smooth boulevards of Paris, and even more exhilarating.

It took us about an hour to get to Gaillon, a charming village a few miles down the left bank of the Seine from Vernon. When we arrived at the racetrack, it was already buzzing with activity. The first race was due to start in only ten minutes' time.

"Come along, everyone, hurry up!" cried Mme. Monet, climbing down from the 937-YZ. "We mustn't miss the start."

The others were obviously too slow for her liking. I was standing with her, waiting for them, when suddenly she caught hold of my hand and whisked me away through the crowds.

"They can follow at their own pace," she told me. "At least *we* shan't miss any of the action!"

She rushed on, and it was all I could do to keep from tripping over my skirts. Somehow I stayed on my feet, gasping apologies to the crowd as we forced our way through it. And then we were right up against a fence at the side of the track, level with the starting line. Mme. Monet, it was clear, knew the layout of the place as if she'd designed it.

Four cars were drawn up with their engines rumbling, ready for the start. A man on the far side of the track raised a flag, held it poised, then brought it down with a flourish. The race was on!

Suddenly the air was filled with dust and gasoline fumes. My eyes watered and I began to cough. It was madly exciting, but I wished we weren't *quite* so close to the starting line! Mme. Monet didn't mind at all. She waved and cheered till the cars were specks in the distance.

"Oh, Paris," she said—it was the first time she'd called me that, and I was pleased—"Paris, isn't the modern world wonderful? The freedom cars give you, the speed!"

Her enthusiasm was infectious. "I know," I said. "It's even more thrilling when you're driving one."

"*You* can drive?" she exclaimed.

"Well . . . yes." Although my skills were debatable, I *had* driven and felt entitled to say so.

"Oh, how fortunate you are!" cried Mme. Monet. "How I wish I could learn . . . but I'm much too old for it now. If only I were as young as you."

"It has nothing to do with age," I told her, suddenly wishing she could have a chance behind the wheel. "It's not hard. It's . . ."

I was drowned out by the sounds of the approaching racers. The lead car had come roaring around the bend and into the home stretch. At

the finish line a man leaned forward with the checkered flag raised.

Mme. Monet was cheering again. "It's the Benz—I knew it! The Benz always wins the speed trials. The others are miles behind. Hurrah for the Benz!"

The flag swished down. The Benz rolled to a halt. Its driver pushed up his goggles and waved, and the crowd went wild.

"It's Georges!" Mme. Monet cried. "Bravo, Georges!"

At once the spectators were out of their seats. I was watching them surge toward the winner when I felt a terrific yank on my arm.

"Come, Paris. This is the time when the spectators can examine the cars!" Mme. Monet's eyes were absolutely alight as we made a beeline for the Benz.

In no time at all we had cut through the crowd and were standing beside Georges, who for his part seemed delighted to see Mme. Monet.

He took her hand, held it briefly to his lips, and said, "Good afternoon, madame. It's been a long time since we've had the pleasure."

"Yes, too long. But all that will change now. We have a car of our own. Not a racer, you understand. A Panhard-Levassor. We shan't be slaves to the train any longer.

"Georges, may I introduce my young friend, Mademoiselle Paris MacKenzie, from the United States. Paris, meet Georges Savel."

"Enchanted, mademoiselle," the young man said, smiling. He raised my hand to his lips.

"Georges," Mme. Monet rushed on, "Paris is already an experienced driver. What do you think of that?"

I opened my mouth to protest, but she didn't give me a chance.

"I wondered if, as a special favor to me, you would let her take the Benz around the track? With myself as passenger, of course."

My stomach lurched. I'd driven a car twice, but I wouldn't have called myself a *driver*. Not on a racetrack!

"But of course," said Georges.

I could have swooned.

"The next race isn't for half an hour. I'll come with you, just in case of difficulties. Though I'm sure mademoiselle will manage perfectly," he added politely.

It was a four-seater, quite a bit bigger than the one I'd driven, but a glance at the controls told me that it wasn't very different to steer. My initial attack of nerves dissolved as if by magic, and then rising excitement was all I felt.

After that, everything happened in a whirl. I was in the driving seat, with a man's cap, back to front, in place of my hat. Georges had placed his own goggles around my forehead, and I pulled them down before thrusting my arms into the big gloves. Georges settled in next to me, and Mme. Monet sat behind. People were clapping and cheering. I couldn't resist giving them a wave.

Now if I could only remember how to start the thing. "I spin the flywheel, don't I?" I said to Georges.

"That's it."

I reached outside and felt the wheel mounted there. I gave it a hard spin and the engine started at once.

Encouraged, I pressed the lever for releasing the brakes, and we moved slowly forward. I could feel the Benz straining to be off. In no time at all I'd steered it into the middle of the track. The way ahead was completely clear.

"Come on, Paris!" Mme. Monet urged. "We can go much faster than this!"

I pressed down on the accelerator and we shot forward. Within moments we were traveling at what must have been a fantastic rate, though it didn't seem so bad with the wide track all to ourselves. There was no need to slow down or worry about steering, except at the turns. Faster and faster we went, with Mme. Monet's excited shrieks spurring me on. I was crouching low over the wheel, looking neither left nor right— just concentrating on the dusty track. It was the greatest sensation of my life.

I saw a blur of people ahead on both sides. From the corner of my eye I caught the swish of the checkered flag and then we whizzed across the finish line.

"We've won!" shouted Mme. Monet. "Bravo, Paris. We've won!"

What did it matter if ours was the only car in the race?

I pressed gently down on the brake pedal, and the Benz rolled to a halt. Mme. Monet was still cheering wildly and even Georges said *"Formidable!"* as he helped me down.

A crowd surrounded the car almost immediately. Somehow Marcel made his way through.

He looked at me, shook his head, and broke out laughing.

"What's so funny?" I demanded, lifting my goggles.

"I don't know whether I'm more impressed by your driving or relieved that I wasn't in the car, but you've certainly given us all a day to remember. Especially Mme. Monet. Look at her."

She was walking with her husband. For the first time since we'd met, she looked completely at ease.

"Do you still think she had something to do with Laroche's death?" asked Marcel.

"I don't know," I admitted. "She's so different today. So happy and animated. I think I'm going to take advantage of her good mood."

"Paris . . ." Marcel's tone was a warning, but I broke off from him and headed toward the Monets. My timing was nearly perfect. Just as I reached them Jean-Pierre approached, said something to Monet, and the two men went off

together, leaving Mme. Monet on her own.

"Madame," I said, taking her arm. "I was wondering if I might ask you a question."

"You might indeed," she said, smiling.

"It's not about cars. It's about . . . madame, would you tell me why you fired Antoine Laroche?"

For an awful moment she froze, and I feared the withdrawn woman I'd first met had returned. Then she smiled with perfect good cheer and said, "Do you know what I have planned for dinner? Roast lamb marinated in olive oil and seasoned with lemon, cinnamon, and a sprig of mint. It's a specialty of Maison du Pressoir."

"Madame," I began again. "About the carpenter—"

"Monsieur Fleury," she called out, cutting me off. Marcel was there in an instant, probably afraid I'd mortally offended our hostess. I barely stifled a groan as she continued her description of the dinner menu to him. Clearly, I wasn't going to get my answer.

"Tell me," she was earnestly asking Marcel, "which is your favorite dinner wine?"

"That's easy," I said, unable to resist. "His favorite is your local specialty—*cailloutin.*"

"Then we shall have it tonight!" she declared.

Marcel grinned at me and said in English, "Paris, I owe you for that."

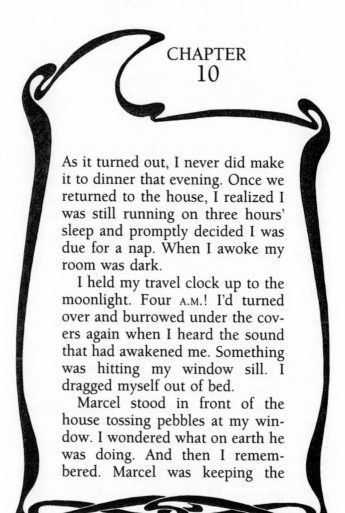

CHAPTER
10

As it turned out, I never did make it to dinner that evening. Once we returned to the house, I realized I was still running on three hours' sleep and promptly decided I was due for a nap. When I awoke my room was dark.

I held my travel clock up to the moonlight. Four A.M.! I'd turned over and burrowed under the covers again when I heard the sound that had awakened me. Something was hitting my window sill. I dragged myself out of bed.

Marcel stood in front of the house tossing pebbles at my window. I wondered what on earth he was doing. And then I remembered. Marcel was keeping the watch we'd agreed on. He'd been up all night. Now it was my turn.

I signaled that I was coming down and dressed quickly. No more running around in a dressing gown, thank you. This time I was dressing for espionage. First I put on a dark brown dress and then chose a dark wool shawl to conceal my light hair. The important thing, I decided, was to wear my galoshes just in case I encountered another dew-soaked field.

Properly dressed, I made my way out of the house. Marcel was just winding up for another throw. I lost no time in pulling him into the shadows.

"Did it take you long to wake me?" I whispered.

"A while. I wanted to let you sleep, but I've already nodded off twice out here myself."

"Haven't you seen anything?"

"Only the bugs. . . . Paris, why are you wearing galoshes?"

"Because . . . oh, never mind!" Even though we were talking in whispers, it was making me nervous. I was sure half the household could hear us. "You've been up long enough. Go on, get some sleep."

I was already heading off when Marcel pulled me back.

He said, "Just a minute. There's something we still have to settle."

"What?"

"The small matter of the wine that was served at dinner. A meal *you* conveniently missed."

"Now, Marcel, it was you who said *cailloutin* was 'a must for visitors.' " I backed away, trying not to laugh, but I couldn't help myself. "Was it really awful?"

"Equal parts vinegar and kerosene," he said. "And they all watched in polite fascination as I drank it." His grimace was comical.

"My poor Marcel," I said, kissing him lightly on the cheek. "Forgive me."

"I'll consider it." Then his eyes grew serious. He took my hands. "Promise me you'll be careful."

I nodded. Then, with a soft "good night," he left me standing in the garden.

It took a moment to get back into the espionage frame of mind. Sherlock Holmes would never have let himself be distracted this way, I told myself sternly as I hid behind my favorite yew tree.

As Marcel had said, only the bugs were active that night. The Maison du Pressoir lay dark and quiet, and it was beginning to occur to me that this watch was totally useless. Still, I was too stubborn to give up. I sat there as the sky changed from black to slate-gray.

It must have been about an hour before daybreak when I heard a creaking noise come from the side of the house. The hothouse door swung open and Mme. Monet emerged, her arms full of

flowers, dressed again in black. She made straight for the *grande allée* and walked very calmly and deliberately down the lane. I had the impression that I was watching some sort of strange ritual.

I waited until I judged she was a safe distance beyond me and then began following. For the umpteenth time I vowed that one day I would learn how to walk soundlessly. As it was, she was nearly out of sight before I trusted myself to get closer.

It was a strange path that Mme. Monet took—across the tracks, over the bridge, through the water garden, and into the meadow beyond. Soon we were no longer on the Monet property.

Mme. Monet continued on for what must have been well over a mile. We were heading away from the center of Giverny, taking the narrow, dirt cow paths that wound through the fields. I knew I would have to stick close to her if I was ever to find my way back. Considering that the villagers so disliked outsiders, I did not fancy being lost in their countryside.

At last we came to a rise, and Mme. Monet's black-clad figure disappeared over the hill. I scrambled after her.

When I got to the top, Mme. Monet was nowhere in sight, and yet I knew exactly where she was. I was facing a stone wall about four feet high, its metal gate slightly ajar. Treetops and a stone cross or two could be seen inside its perimeter. A badly weathered sign read CIMETIÈRE DE GIVERNY—Giverny Cemetery.

I crouched next to the wall so that I could just see over its edge. Madame Monet made her way between the tombstones. Then she knelt by one of the fresher graves. I couldn't see her face beneath her shawl—she was turned away from me—but the sound of her crying carried clearly through the early morning stillness. Very gently she took faded flowers from a brass urn and replaced them with the ones she'd brought. She kept smoothing the mound with her hands, as if trying to comfort whoever lay beneath.

I sank down onto the ground beside the wall, overcome with shame. "I should not be here," I thought. The poor woman had the right to mourn in privacy. Knowing that her terrible grief explained her erratic behavior, and Monet's efforts to shield her from the murder, only made me feel worse. I had been terribly insensitive. As she cried I only wished that I could think of a way to comfort her.

After some time Madame's sobbing stopped and I heard the cemetery gate close. Then she passed down the hill and out of sight.

Although I had lost all enthusiasm for it, I knew I had to finish what I had started. And so I crept into the cemetery and began to search for the grave with its urn of freshly cut flowers.

It didn't take long to find. The name on the stone was that of a Suzanne Butler, who'd died a

little over a year ago, in February of 1899. She was identified as being the wife of Samuel, mother of Lily, and "beloved daughter of Alice Hoschedé Monet."

CHAPTER
11

I couldn't remember the complicated maze of cow paths I'd taken to the cemetery, so I just struck out in what I felt was the right direction. It didn't help that the sky was still deep gray. The sun was doing its level best to rise, but it didn't have a chance against the dark, heavy clouds that were gathering. It was clear that I didn't have long before a storm broke, and my journey had already taken twice as long as it should have. I was also beginning to worry that one of the local farmers might find me thrashing my way through his fields.

Thankfully, just as a fine, cold rain began to fall, I caught sight of the Monet land. The boundary of the water garden was just ahead, and that meant I was as good as in my room. Or so I thought.

Even in the rain the water garden was beautiful, and I was enraptured enough to stop and admire it. Then I noticed him. Clothed entirely in black, a hooded figure was untying the small skiff that Monet kept moored to the bank, west of the bridge.

The letter! I'd never shown it to Monet, or the police for that matter, and now the saboteur was here in the garden about to make good on his threats! Well, I'd just have to stop him—though exactly how I was going to accomplish that was anybody's guess. I crouched down in the wet grass and inched forward.

As I said, before I become a really first-class sleuth, I'll have to learn to move silently. I couldn't have gone more than two inches before the saboteur whipped his head around in my direction. A chill ran through me as I saw that except for tiny eye and nose slits, the hood completely covered his face. He'd made himself a figure of pure darkness, something out of a gothic tale. I prayed as I had never prayed before that he hadn't seen me.

There was an extremely long moment when both of us remained frozen. And then, to my horror, he began to move toward me. I snapped. Before I realized I was doing it, I was up and running madly for the bridge. All ideas of stop-

ping him were gone. I knew only that I had to get to the house.

He took off after me. I screamed as loudly as I could, hoping that one of the gardeners might be awake. Though I didn't dare look, I could hear him behind me. He was fast. He wasn't wearing a soaking-wet ankle-length skirt or galoshes, and he was gaining on me. As I felt him close the last yard between us, I darted to the side, hoping he'd at least lose some momentum. It was a perfectly decent strategy; the only problem was that it didn't work. When I moved sideways I slid on the wet grass and landed hard on my side.

A gloved hand clamped over my mouth. His other arm went under my knees and lifted me up. Though I was kicking like a mule, it seemed to have no effect on him. He carried me easily toward the stream, and a vision of Antoine's floating dead body flashed before me.

I struggled even more wildly, and he responded by crushing me so hard against his chest that I could barely move. He wasn't very tall, but he had the strength of someone who'd worked with his body all his life.

He carried me away from the bridge toward the area where the lily pond widened and got deeper. I felt my throat constrict with pure terror as he waded out into the water. He stopped exactly at the midpoint, where the water swirled around his hips.

Calm down, I told myself. You've got to knock him off balance. My stomach lurched as I tried to predict whether he'd use his knife or simply hold me under until I drowned.

He did neither. The saboteur dropped me unceremoniously into the stream, as if he was suddenly bored with holding me. I sank, flailed around underwater for a minute or so, and then surfaced, spluttering. The man in black was gone.

To make a long story short, I'll simply say that I returned to the house in a torrential downpour, sloshed up the stairs undiscovered, emptied at least a quart of water out of each of my galoshes, and put myself to bed.

It was ten thirty in the morning before I awoke, and I probably would have gone on sleeping if I hadn't been so thirsty. I sat up to get out of bed and stopped right there. My side was aching from the fall I'd taken and my back was stiff. Worse, my throat was sore and my nose stuffy. What with two nights of running around soaking wet, I had the beginnings of a splendid cold.

The rain was still coming down outside, and all I wanted to do was to spend the day under the covers, sipping hot tea. But I needed to show Monet the letter, tell him of my run-in with the saboteur, see if I could find out why Antoine had been fired, and—oh, no—how could anyone model with a head cold?

There was a sharp rapping on my door. "Who is it?" I called.

"Are you all right?" Marcel called back.

I put on my dressing gown and opened the door a crack. "What are you doing here?" I whispered.

"The last time I saw you, you were standing in the garden in the middle of the night. When you didn't come down this morning, I—"

"I'm all right," I assured him. "But you can't stay here. Madame Monet already thinks you are too forward with me."

Marcel pushed open the door. "You look terrible," he said.

"Thanks."

"I didn't mean it that way. . . . Paris, you'd better tell me what happened last night." With that, he stepped inside, closed the door behind him, and sat down in the chair by the window.

For once I was concerned about what was proper. "Please, Marcel. If anyone finds out you're in here—"

"I'll tell them I thought you might not be feeling well when you didn't show up for breakfast and came to check on you. You're *not* feeling well, are you?"

He was worse than my mother, and she's a doctor!

"I think I have a head cold. I got caught in the rain."

"Do you want me to go down and get you some tea? Or some fruit and toast?"

"No. There's too much to do today. If Madame Monet finds out I'm sick, she may not let me out." I poured a glass of water from the blue ceramic pitcher on the washstand. "I'll get dressed and come down for lunch." With that I got back into bed, drew my knees up, and pulled the quilt up over them.

"Well, you should know what's been going on this morning. The entire household has been in an uproar."

"Why?" I wondered if the saboteur had finished his work after disposing of me.

"It's raining."

"Is that all?"

"Apparently it's everything. Monet can't go outside to paint, so he's gone back to bed. That is, after he spent the better part of breakfast storming around, glaring at the skies as if he could scare them into sunshine. Madame Monet is with him, trying to comfort him, but she's as depressed as he is furious, so you can just imagine . . ."

I couldn't help laughing.

"One good thing came of it," he continued with a smile. "When they went upstairs, I was left alone with Jean-Pierre. He finally explained why his mother has acted so strangely, and why they're all so frantic not to upset her."

"Suzanne's death?"

Marcel looked at me sharply. "How did you know?"

"Last night I followed Madame Monet to the cemetery. It was so awful, Marcel. She's completely broken up by it. She just knelt by the grave crying. And there I was—spying on her! I didn't know what to do, so I just hid. And . . . and later when I came back . . ." I felt myself trembling as I saw it all again. "I ran into the saboteur." I put my head down on my knees. "He didn't hurt me, but I think he's the murderer. I could just feel it."

Marcel came over to the bed. "Move over," he said gently. Then he sat down next to me, put an arm around my shoulders, and held me. For a long while we just sat like that, listening to the rain.

By the time the lunch bell rang, I was lacing up my boots and feeling better. The aches had subsided. More important, I'd told Marcel everything, and that had somehow restored my spirits. The next step was to get Monet alone, give him the letter, and tell him what had happened in the water garden. The question was, how could I tell him about the saboteur without admitting I'd been spying on his wife? I could hear the conversation already: "You see, sir, it was about six thirty in the morning and I couldn't sleep and I thought, what a perfectly delightful rainstorm! Why don't I take a stroll in the water

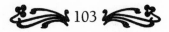

garden . . ." Relax, I told myself as I straightened the ivory silk blouse I'd put on. You'll think of something. Then, giving my skirt a last tug, I went down to lunch.

Once again everyone was seated by the time I arrived—even Marcel. This is beginning to look like a habit, I realized uneasily. The last thing I needed was to irritate Monet by coming late to meals. Never had I seen a household that ran on such a strict schedule!

Fortunately, Monet didn't seem to notice my tardiness. He was staring intently at the vase of delphiniums on the table.

Mme. Monet asked, "Are you well, Paris? We missed you at breakfast."

"I'm fine, thanks. It felt like a good day for sleeping." Immediately I saw that I'd said the wrong thing.

"It is *not* a good day," Monet told me quite firmly. "Much too dark, and this rain—how am I supposed to paint?"

I was tempted to suggest that he paint inside, like every other artist, but held my tongue.

He regarded me carefully for a moment, then broke into a broad smile. We were in for another lightning change of personality. "I know exactly what you are thinking, young lady. Why this mania for painting outside? Well, I'll tell you. What is painted outdoors, on the spot, has a force and power that can't be matched by anything painted in the studio. In fact, since I don't

choose to spend the day in bed, I shall go into the studio anyway and touch up some paintings I did last month. . . . You haven't seen the second studio yet, have you?"

"No," I said, "only the rooms in the house."

"Then you and Monsieur Fleury shall accompany me, and I will show you what I mean."

This was even better than I'd hoped. "That would be wonderful," I told him.

After dessert Marcel and I accompanied Monet to the old farm building that had been converted to his new studio. The rain had let up, so I wondered if Monet would change his mind and set off alone for the water garden. But the skies were still very gray, and he kept muttering things like "To be sure I need a dark sky, but not *this* dark" and "Filthy weather!"

The studio, a big squarish building, lay beyond a grove of lime trees. "I had this redone a year ago," Monet explained as he opened the wooden door. "There's not much of interest on the ground floor—a darkroom, the gardener's quarters, and the garage for the 937-YZ." He was already climbing a rather steep flight of stairs. Marcel was behind him, and I followed, marveling at the brisk pace Monet set.

"Here we are," he said, ushering us through a doorway at the head of the stairs. "My second studio."

It was a spacious room, very sparely furnished. The only items of any size were a rolltop desk and a vitrine full of Japanese ceramics.

Despite the overcast weather, the studio seemed flooded with light. Monet had had an immense window set in the north wall, and the south wall had been rebuilt to form a glazed balcony overlooking the greenhouse. As in the first studio, the walls were covered with his work, and rows of canvases lay stacked against the walls. Brilliant, luminous patterns of sun and shadow, here were the gardens of Giverny as they changed throughout the year. The paintings took my breath away.

Monet lit a cigarette and began rifling impatiently through a row of canvases. At last he found what he'd been looking for—a small painting, a detail of the branches of a willow tree.

"This," he said, holding it up against the window. "I painted it here. It's a detail from that large one on the wall." He nodded to a study of the bridge.

Then he said to Marcel, "There's a knife on the desk. Would you hand it to me?"

Marcel gave him the knife, and without another word Monet proceeded to rip the canvas to shreds.

"What are you doing?" I cried.

Monet regarded me calmly. "I have just ripped up the canvas, mademoiselle."

"I know, but—"

"And soon I shall make a fire and burn it as it

deserves. It was poor work. That it was not painted from life would be evident to a child."

It hadn't been evident to me, but what I said was, "You might have sold it."

"Of course I could have sold it! These days the general opinion holds that any painting of mine is a masterpiece. Flattering, but ridiculous. I produce my share of rubbish, the same as anyone else. Who then would destroy it if I didn't do it myself?"

Neither one of us attempted to answer the question.

Monet stood in front of a medium-sized view of the bridge that was heavy with deep greens and browns. "Do you think this is too dark?" he asked me. It was by far the darkest painting there.

"No," I said truthfully. There was something in the mood of the painting that captured exactly the way the garden had felt to me that morning—shadowy and dangerous and yet still unbelievably beautiful.

"I do," Monet said brusquely. "I will tell you something. I am afraid of the dark. Even when I am the one putting it on canvas, I see death in it."

A chill ran through me. It was almost as if through the painting Monet had foreseen that the paradise he created would also contain evil.

Marcel must have been thinking the same thing, for he said, "Monsieur, could we talk for a moment about Antoine Laroche?"

Monet sighed heavily and sat himself on a tall stool. "Go ahead."

"We went to the *gendarmerie,* as you asked," Marcel began, and then he told Monet of the photo chemical and splinters on Antoine's body. "Does that mean anything to you?"

"Very little, I'm afraid. As you have undoubtedly noticed, I spend all my time either with my paintings or my family. I respect the people who work here, naturally, but I'm afraid I don't know them very well."

I decided I had to risk asking. "The police also told us that Madame Monet fired Antoine on the morning of his death. Do you know anything about that?"

Monet looked troubled. "There, too, I am ignorant. It is Alice who keeps this household running, and . . ." Again he read the unasked question on my face. "No, I haven't asked her why." He sighed. "I think you both deserve an explanation. A little more than a year ago, my wife lost her daughter. Suzanne had been sick for five years—an agonizing paralysis contracted after her daughter, Lily, was born. Still, Suzanne's death came as a terrible shock. Alice loved her dearly. We all did, and each of us has had to come to terms with the loss in our own way.

"My plans for extending the lily pool have taken up much of my attention; that and my

painting have distracted me from my sorrow. The younger ones have natural resilience, which has enabled them to overcome their grief. But my dear Alice has given in to deep melancholy, and it has become her constant companion."

"I'm sorry, Monsieur Monet."

"As am I. Reason, logic—they do no good in the face of such intense feelings. It is painful to us all to watch her feeding them further by going to the cemetery every morning, in all weather, to brood at Suzanne's grave. She summons me home from painting trips with wild, frightening letters. And any mention of death in her hearing is enough to send her into hysterics."

"Then that's why she couldn't be told of Laroche's death?" said Marcel.

"That and no other reason, I assure you. She was deeply distressed at having to dismiss him. You can imagine what the news of his death would have done."

"Monsieur Monet," I said, "I think she may *have* to be told. The police need all the help they can get."

I handed him the saboteur's letter. Monet read it and set it on the desk. "It is not important," he said, his voice expressionless.

"I mean no disrespect," Marcel said quickly, "but you are wrong, monsieur. It is possible that Antoine Laroche died because he tried to prevent the saboteur from destroying your irises. If

that is true and the saboteur returns, then everyone in your household risks a confrontation with a murderer. You must show the police this letter. They must find out whatever they can about what happened to Laroche on the morning of his death."

Monet was emphatic. "No! There has been sabotage before, but never personal harm to anyone here. I think Laroche's death was an accident. And as for dealing with the sabotage, I will do what I have done in the past—ignore it! Going to the police would only make things worse. I do not need to incite the villagers further by threatening them with arrest."

Marcel looked at me in dismay, and I knew I had to tell Monet what had happened that morning—even if I did leave out certain pertinent details. I said, "Did you know that the saboteur returned to your water garden early this morning?"

"What? Impossible. Duran would have noticed any damage."

"He didn't damage anything this time only because he didn't get a chance," I said, wincing at the memory. "I saw him. Early this morning, I . . . I'd been lying in bed, thinking about all this, and . . . and I got an impulse to go back to the water garden. I nearly always follow my impulses, so at about six thirty I went out and—"

"You want out alone at that hour in the rain?" Monet asked. "Even if you felt you had to go,

which I do not understand at all, why didn't you have someone accompany you? Surely one of the servants—"

"Monsieur," Marcel cut in smoothly, "you are dealing with a most independent young lady. An American, also. Questions of the sort you just asked are entirely useless. Believe me, I know."

I silently thanked Marcel. "What matters," I went on, "is what I found out there." And then I told him of the saboteur.

Monet heard me out. When I finished he went to the window, and then, as if searching for something there and not finding it, he turned to his canvases. "In my water garden," he said finally. "In my water garden." He turned to me. "You are right. It is much more serious than I'd thought. I cannot tell you how sorry I am for what happened this morning, but . . . I will do what I can. Tonight, I will tell Alice of Laroche's death and ask her about him. She must hear of it sooner or later, and better from me than from others." He paused for a moment. "Would the two of you be willing to dine at the hotel this evening?"

"Of course, monsieur," Marcel replied.

"Thank you. You see, there will be a painful scene when I tell her, and it would be better if only the family were here."

"And the letter?" I asked. "Will you show it to the police?"

"I don't know, mademoiselle. You will have to

let me think about that and trust my decision."

"We should let you return to your painting," Marcel said.

"Indeed." Monet smiled at us with genuine warmth. "I know I am not the ideal host—a temperamental old man obsessed with splattering paint on canvas. But this obsession . . . how can I explain it to you? . . . The very first time I came to Giverny, I was so thunderstruck by what I saw that I could not be aware of anything else." He chuckled. "And, my friends, it has been that way ever since."

CHAPTER
12

At two o'clock that afternoon I checked myself in the mirror. I had on a high-necked white dress trimmed with lace. I'd already tried on every other dress and skirt I'd brought, and my bed was covered with rejects. The white was pretty, but it felt too formal. What did one wear to model, anyway? I had to find something *perfect* so that Devereaux wouldn't even dream of asking me to put on a sheet.

Maybe the red wool would be better? No. It was really too warm for that. I took off the white, stared at the bed, and in a fit of desperation put on what I'd originally worn that morning, an ivory silk blouse with a lavender skirt. It

would have to do, I decided. And now there was still my face and hair to make presentable. After about two seconds I realized this was impossible. I simply could not make my face look glamorous when my nose was stuffy. Accepting this law of the universe, I set out for my appointment with Devereaux.

Now that I no longer suspected the Monets, it seemed more important than ever that I get into Antoine Laroche's house. I had a feeling that the key to the puzzle lay in N° 13, rue des Chandeliers. And as the dilapidated old house came into view, my heart began to pound.

N° 13 looked even worse than I remembered. The path to the door was almost completely overgrown with nettles. I lifted my skirt a little and picked my way among them. The doorbell, I was glad to find, was still in working order.

Devereaux opened the door and flashed me a dazzling smile. "Paris! I'm so glad you came. I was afraid you might change your mind."

"I always keep my word," I told him.

"Well, then enter my abode."

His "abode" made Monet's studio seem cluttered. The large main room was completely unfurnished save for a wooden armchair, an easel, and a small stand that held a palette and paints. Faded ivory curtains were drawn shut, and I wondered fleetingly why Devereaux bothered with full-length curtains when there were no other signs of human comfort in the room. There

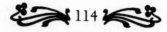

were three doors in the far wall, all of them closed.

Like Monet, Devereaux had stacks of canvases propped up against the walls. The walls themselves were bare, unless you counted as decoration the rather interesting pattern of peeling paint. There was nothing to suggest Antoine Laroche had ever been here.

"I did say it was humble," Devereaux offered. He looked me over with a practiced eye. "You look lovely," he said. "That blouse is very becoming."

"Thank you."

"Unfortunately, it is not exactly how I want to paint you. Wait here a moment." He disappeared behind the door on the left and returned a few minutes later, holding a large paper bag. "I'd like you to change into this," he said, thrusting it toward me.

A sheet! I thought with dismay. "Uh . . . no. I mean, I can't."

"Why ever not?"

"Because . . ."

"Paris, you don't have to model for me if you don't want to," said Devereaux. "But if you do, please wear something I want to paint."

I took a deep breath and reached out for the bag.

"Good. You can change in that room behind you."

Well, I thought, at least I'm getting to see

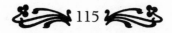

more of the house. But the room he sent me into was empty. And that left only the bag to concentrate on.

If the sheet is too skimpy, I'll tell him I have a cold and can't risk a chill, I resolved. But inside the bag was something made of coarse indigo-blue material—a smock; and beneath it a homespun blouse. It was the least glamorous outfit I'd ever seen. Devereaux was dressing me like a Giverny field hand! Not only was I extremely relieved, I was a little insulted. I changed quickly, laid the bag on the floor, and folded my own clothes on top of it.

Devereaux's eyes lit up when he saw me, and that seemed reward enough for getting dressed in this horrible outfit. "Giverny could use a milkmaid who looks like you," he said.

"Of all the things I could possibly wear . . ."

"Ever since I came here, I've been wanting to paint the villagers," he explained, "but you know how they feel about it. There is not one of them who will pose for me. Sit down, please."

I sat down on the chair, and Devereaux scrutinized me from every angle. At last he said, "Put your left hand on the armrest and see if you can tilt your chin a little to the right. Good. Do you think you can remember how that position feels, holding your head just so?"

"I guess."

"Then relax while I prepare the paints."

He squeezed patches of blue, yellow, green,

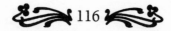

and white onto his palette and carefully blended drops of each. In a few minutes he'd duplicated the blue of the smock perfectly.

"All right," he said when he'd added some other colors to the palette. "We're ready to start. Can you go back to that position?"

"I'll try," I said, arranging myself as best I could.

"Now, you can talk if you like, and let me know whenever you want a break, but try not to shift your body or head."

I nodded, then froze when I realized I'd moved. This was going to be much harder than I thought!

Fortunately, Devereaux was entertaining. He told me funny stories about the farm he'd grown up on, asked me about America, and was full of questions about what I'd been doing in Giverny.

I wasn't about to tell him that I'd been searching for a murderer, so instead I described the races at Gaillon.

"Next portrait, I paint you in goggles," he promised. Then he asked, "Tell me, does the great Monet ever go to the races?"

"Of course. Though it's his wife who's the real fan."

"I didn't think he ever left his canvases," said Devereaux somewhat bitterly.

I turned to look at him, surprised by his tone of voice.

"Paris!" he snapped. "Your head!"

"Sorry." I readjusted. "Devereaux, do you remember when we first met at the train station?"

"I will never forget."

"You said something then, about how I might prefer staying in town rather than at the *Maison*. Why?"

He shrugged. "Monet is very aloof, very moody. Of all the artists here, there are only about five he will even speak to. I'd love to study with him, but I don't think I could share the same roof. And now with Antoine's death . . . there must be police all over the place."

"You'd think so."

He looked at me with interest. "No investigation?"

"Well, there is, but . . ." For some reason I didn't want to go into it. "The police haven't told us much."

Neither of us said anything for a long while. I sat, concentrating on remaining still, and then on Devereaux. Today he was wearing a jacket of dark burgundy, paint-splattered but dashing all the same. He worked intently, using three different brushes, pausing now and then to wipe his hands on a rag that stuck out of his back pocket. I was so curious about what was on the canvas!

"Want a break?" he asked.

I got up and stretched gratefully while he cleaned the brushes with turpentine.

This was my chance to look around. "I've got the start of a cold, and I'm thirsty," I said. "If you'll just point me toward the kitchen, I'll get a glass of water."

"I'll get it," he said, and before I could protest, he disappeared through the center door.

That left me only one option. Moving as quietly as I could, I opened the door on the right. It didn't lead to a room at all, but to a narrow hallway with a staircase at the end. Like everything I'd seen here so far, the hallway was completely empty. Well, not quite. A large, black leather box sat at the foot of the stairs.

"Curious?" I nearly jumped out of my skin at the sound of his voice.

"You scared me!"

"I didn't mean to." He held out the water to me and, when I'd taken it, firmly closed the door to the hallway. "The upstairs is where Laroche had his rooms," he said, leading me back to the chair. "He used to pace for hours at night. Even now I think I still hear that infernal ceiling creaking. . . . How about one more sitting? I just want to finish the outline."

I sat down, managed to remember the position, and vowed that I'd never do this again. Modeling is for people who are good at sitting still. That is definitely *not* one of my talents.

"Does Monet still do most of his painting outside?" Devereaux asked.

"As much as he can. This morning's weather did not please him."

Devereaux laughed. "I'll bet it didn't," he said,

almost to himself.

Something was wrong, I thought. But what was it? Something Devereaux had said? I glanced at him, and his response was instantaneous.

"Will you stop squirming!" He wasn't yelling, but he'd gone white with anger.

"I'm sorry!" I exclaimed, a little taken aback. "I've never done this before!"

"No, of course you haven't." His voice softened. "I'm sorry. Really. It's just that it's been so long since I've worked with a model, I'm a little overeager. Come here and I'll show you what I've done, and then we'll call it a day."

It was mostly an outline of what the painting would be, I saw, though he had started to fill in part of one shoulder.

"It's a slow process," said Devereaux, "but now that the outline is done it will go faster. Will you come again tomorrow . . . perhaps at one?"

I was tempted to say no, as by now the idea of having my portrait done had lost its appeal. I weighed this against losing my chance to find any clues to the mystery here. And then I realized what had been bothering me. Yesterday, Devereaux had said that Antoine was almost never in the house; today he'd complained of his "infernal" pacing. How could a man who was never here irritate Devereaux that way? My skin prickled and I felt a rush of bright awareness. Suddenly I knew that the key to the mystery was

Louis Devereaux. I had no choice now.

"I'll be here tomorrow at one," I said.

That evening, as we had promised Monet, Marcel and I went to the hotel to dine. After dark it seemed that the hotel changed character—it was no longer lackluster, but brightly lit and lively. As we approached, a group of horse-drawn carriages pulled up and a half dozen young men, all quite elegant in evening dress, stepped down and walked into the hotel. I took Marcel's arm as we entered. In his black evening suit he was quite the handsomest man there.

Mme. Baudy was at the reception desk, writing in a ledger. She smiled when she saw us. "The restaurant is that way," she said, pointing past the bar. *"Bon appétit."*

I suppose that for a Normandy village the restaurant was pretty grand; it boasted red plush banquettes, chandeliers, and even a small orchestra. Paintings of every size and standard covered the walls. I wondered briefly if any of them were the work of Devereaux. Certainly, there was not a Monet among them.

When the waiter came to take our order, I asked if the paintings were all by local artists.

"Oh, yes," he assured me.

"How did so many of them come to be here?" Marcel asked.

"As payment for bills, I expect. Madame Baudy's a kind-hearted soul. She can't bring herself to press anyone who's down to his last sou."

That was interesting. Devereaux had claimed that he'd had to move out of the hotel because Mme. Baudy's demands had become exorbitant. Either Devereaux was lying, or he'd been a disagreeable tenant. Devereaux again! Why was it I hadn't been able to stop thinking about him? He was handsome and charming, true, but more important, he was a man with a secret. And I had to know what it was.

After we ordered, Marcel said, "What is that expression in your country? A penny for your thoughts?"

"You're going to say, 'I told you so.' "

"Let me guess . . . there is something about Louis Devereaux that makes you uneasy."

I nodded as the waiter returned with our entrées. The veal cooked in wine sauce with mushrooms smelled heavenly.

"Well, don't feel too bad," Marcel said. "Devereaux made me uneasy, too, the first time I met him. Only . . . I chalked it up to jealousy. What happened there today? Did you find anything?"

"I didn't get to see very much—only the living room, where he was painting, a little room in the back, and a glimpse of the hallway that led upstairs."

"And?"

"Either he's even poorer than he claims or those rooms were cleaned out. Marcel, I've never seen such a bare, empty house! There was nothing except his art supplies, a big black box in the hall, and . . . he brought me a glass of water, so I suppose he has a kitchen."

"What about Devereaux himself?"

"He nearly lost his temper when I moved." I giggled. "I'm a terrible model. Actually, he was rather nice, but I think he's lying about Madame Baudy and Antoine. . . ."

Marcel listened as I told him what Devereaux had said. "So you think he had something to do with the death?"

"I'm not sure," I admitted. "I think it's more like Madame Monet—he knows something important that he's not telling. I'm going back there at one tomorrow. I want to find out what it is."

"I *don't* think that's a good idea."

"Please don't look so worried," I said. "I don't think Devereaux is dangerous. Now, tell me, what happened in the village? Did you find out anything about that old man who cursed Monet?"

"Well, he certainly doesn't fit the description of the saboteur that you gave me," said Marcel. "And it seems he sprained his ankle shortly after he was so rude to us, so he couldn't have attacked you in the water garden. As for the rest, no one is talking. The saboteur could be anyone—or even more than one person." Marcel picked up his fork. "How's your veal?" he asked.

"Delicious." The waiter poured the wine, then

Marcel and I touched glasses and, by unspoken agreement, set about enjoying dinner. I soon became aware of the other patrons, and again got a thrill out of hearing so many American voices. With the exception of our table, everyone in the restaurant seemed to know everyone else, and there was a great deal of loud, affectionate greeting and conversation.

At a nearby table the talk turned to Monet, and what I heard corroborated what Devereaux had said—there was a mixture of awe and resentment as Monet was discussed. It seemed that everyone in the village—farmer and artist alike—had a reason to dislike him. But how many would be capable of murder?

The night had grown cool by the time Marcel and I left the hotel and set off for the *Maison*. Avoiding the rue des Chandeliers, we made our way up to the center of Giverny. A narrow alley brought us into the square on the side where the police station stood. I took two steps into the open, then froze.

"Stop, Marcel!" I hissed. "Look!"

I pointed to a lithe figure in a green velvet jacket and dark blue trousers hurrying across the far side of the square. Devereaux! He was carrying a large black box and heading for, of all places, the hotel.

"I wouldn't have thought he'd be caught dead

in there," I said. "What could he possibly be up to?"

"Let's wait here till he comes out," Marcel suggested. "Then maybe we can ask Madame Baudy."

We drew back into the alley. After only a few minutes Devereaux reappeared empty-handed, and set off across the square.

"Right," I said. "Let's have a word with Madame Baudy."

The good lady was at her shop counter. She looked, if anything, more startled than ever.

"An extraordinary thing!" she exclaimed, without bothering to exchange greetings. "That Louis Devereaux—worst tenant I ever had. Rude young fellow. Never paid a centime. Had to evict him. Hated to cause trouble, but I had no choice. . . . I'm sorry? Did you ask me for something, mademoiselle?"

She was clearly too agitated to wonder why we had come back.

"Louis Devereaux," I said. "Did he give you anything just now?"

"That's just it! Imagine my surprise. In payment for all the rent he owed. I'd written it off as a bad debt, only he insisted. Charming apology. Touching. Least I could do was tell him he can have his studio back, whenever he wishes. Dear me, how one can misjudge character!"

"He gave you one of his pictures, madame?" asked Marcel.

"No, no. Something of real value."

She reached under the counter and lifted up the black box for us to inspect. I saw at once what it was.

"A camera."

That perplexed me. Devereaux had never mentioned being a photographer.

"He said he had no more use for it," Mme. Baudy continued. "Worth quite a bit, wouldn't you say, monsieur?"

"Undoubtedly, madame," Marcel said. "If you'll excuse us, though, we ought to be hurrying along."

"You *can't* go back to rue des Chandeliers tomorrow" was the first thing Marcel said once we were out on the street.

"What do you mean I can't—"

"Paris, I found traces of photographic chemicals on Laroche's body. Devereaux just gave Madame Baudy his camera—a camera you saw in his house this afternoon."

"True. But it's not uncommon for artists to have cameras. Monet has an entire darkroom! And don't you think the fact that Devereaux was honest enough to finally pay his debt counts for something?"

"If I could only figure out what," Marcel muttered.

"Marcel," I said, "this is more reason than ever for me to go back there. I must find out what Devereaux knows about Antoine."

CHAPTER
13

Early the next morning I awakened to the sound of Monet's voice thundering through the house. Now what? I thought, and sat up to peer through the window. The sun was shining, so he couldn't possibly be raging about the weather. From my room it was impossible to make out what he was saying, only that he was saying it very loudly. I didn't particularly want to go downstairs into the middle of the outburst, but I reasoned that if I got dressed and listened from the top of the staircase, I'd be able to figure out what was going on.

I crept along the hallway. Below, I could see Monet prowling up and down like a caged tiger. Mme.

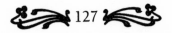

Monet was following at a safe distance, making little soothing sounds which he ignored. And Duran, the gardener, stood well away from both of them, looking very uncomfortable.

There was a sound behind me, and I turned to see Marcel coming down the hallway. Before he could ask what I was doing, I put a finger to my lips. He knelt down beside me, and together we watched the drama below.

The parlor door opened, and Jean-Pierre entered the room. He gave his stepfather a half-hearted smile. "Nothing else was touched, Papa. I have checked everywhere."

"That was very considerate," Monet replied caustically. "I must remember to thank them for showing such restraint."

He was clearly working himself up to the point of another eruption, and it was not long in coming. "How could they do it?" he shouted. "My *nymphéas*! What have I ever done to them? I did not invite all these seventh-rate artists to move here! I do not bother anyone. All I want is to keep to myself and paint. I—"

"Please, Monet!" Mme. Monet sounded desperate.

Monet lowered his voice at once. "Forgive me, Alice," he said gruffly, "but this is too much!" Then, looking rather ashamed of his behavior, he folded her into his arms.

Marcel and I had seen enough. As quietly as we could, we retreated down the hall.

"It's exactly what the letter threatened," I said.

"Yes. And he thought ignoring it would work."

"Maybe now that the water lilies are gone, the sabotage will stop," I suggested hopefully. "The villagers won't have to worry about the water."

Marcel looked skeptical. "Personally, I can't imagine Monet accepting this. I'll bet within a month he has new lilies planted."

Then, despite the tempest that had just gone on, two bells rang. Breakfast was being served.

We were the only ones at the table. A servant told us that Mme. Monet was in her room and Monet had gone out to the orchard to paint. Jean-Pierre had returned to the garden with Duran. It was very strange, just the two of us eating there, but it was also the most comfortable meal I'd had at the Monets'. They were not exactly a relaxing family.

"What's on the agenda today, my dear Holmes?" asked Marcel as we were finishing up. "And please don't suggest I spend another day talking to farmers who don't want to be bothered."

"Actually, my dear Watson, I thought you might talk to some of the artists."

Marcel considered this. "Fair enough, but in the meantime I've got another idea. As a matter of fact, you gave it to me last night when you said that Monet has a darkroom in the second studio. I've been thinking . . . Antoine was hired to help build the second studio. We might find a clue there."

It sounded like a good idea to me, so we set off at once, taking care not to be seen by Monet as we crossed the lime grove. It wasn't hard to avoid his gaze—he was completely absorbed. He sat under the shade of a large umbrella with three easels set up before him, each holding a partially completed painting of the lime trees. Jean-Pierre had told Marcel that Monet would paint on one until the light changed, and then, seeing the scene completely differently, would move to another canvas.

The studio building was deserted. We let ourselves in and spent some time poking around the first floor. I took a good long look at the 937-YZ, because I couldn't resist, while Marcel headed for the darkroom. When I finally tore myself away from the car and joined him, he was holding a glass bottle filled with a clear, yellowish liquid.

"This is it," he said. "But you were right. Anyone who develops photographs would have it. Maybe Devereaux had something to do with Antoine's death, or maybe Antoine was in here. Then again, Antoine could have brushed up against anyone with a camera."

"That's what I like," I told him. "Conclusive evidence."

Marcel grinned, put the bottle down, and took my arm. "Let's take a quick look upstairs, O great sleuth."

We climbed the stairs without talking. I pushed the door open and caught my breath. Today the studio was filled with bright sunlight, and the paintings seemed to shimmer with it. We stepped into the room and, forgetting about Antoine for the moment, let ourselves be overwhelmed by Monet.

"I think it's his eyes," Marcel said at last.

"Whose eyes?"

"I think the way he sees, *what* he sees, is different from the rest of us. He—"

"Marcel, I just noticed something," I said. "Monet's replaced that painting, the dark one."

Marcel came out of his reverie long enough to look toward the place on the wall where I was pointing. "You're right," he said. "This painting is similar, very similar, but the greens are different. In this one the green is . . . more like first spring."

It was. You could feel the change of season and sometimes even the heat of the day in Monet's paintings. But the springtime green wasn't what caught my attention. Instead, I noticed what was missing. There was none of the darkness in this one—none of the danger.

I sat down on Monet's stool, wondering if he often changed the arrangement of paintings on the walls. And then I noticed something else.

I crossed over to the back wall, knelt down, and picked up a small piece of rag. Unsurprisingly, it was splattered with paint.

"What is it?" Marcel asked.

I handed it to him. "Look at the color of the paint."

"It's blue."

"Yes, but do you see this blue anywhere else in the room?"

Marcel gazed at the canvases on the wall and shrugged. "I don't know. Monet uses layer upon layer of color. I'd have to spend hours with a magnifying glass."

"Well, I don't," I said, feeling a little sick. "This is a very specific indigo blue, and it's not Monet's. Don't you see? It's exactly the color of the farmers' smocks."

"Which means . . . ?" Marcel was watching me carefully now.

"Which means I know who the saboteur is. . . . And I was so sure it wasn't him," I added, more to myself than Marcel.

"Devereaux."

"He painted me in one of those blue smocks that the villagers wear," I said. "He matched the color perfectly. And while he was painting, he used a rag to wipe off his hands. . . . Now a painting that was here yesterday isn't here today, and someone's hung a very similar one in its place. This scrap is proof that Devereaux was here."

"You're sure he's the saboteur?" Marcel asked. "He could just be an art thief. The saboteur might be someone else altogether."

"I wish I could believe that. . . ." I stared across the studio. Something from yesterday's session was nagging at me. "Marcel, do you remember what he told Madame Baudy when he gave her the camera?"

"That he wanted to pay his debt."

"No. There was something more . . . that he didn't have any use for it any longer. That's why his rooms were so barren—he *had* cleaned out! I think Devereaux is about to leave town. We've got to stop him!" I looked at my watch. "Devereaux is expecting me to model for him in exactly twenty minutes. I must go."

"You're not going anywhere," said Marcel, planting himself firmly in front of the studio door. "You've just told me you think Devereaux's the saboteur and at the very least has stolen from Monet, and now you say you still want to model for him?"

"If he's really planning to leave town, I may be able to delay him," I said reasonably. "And I can't help it—I still feel as if there's something important in that house that I haven't found. I've got to go."

"Take me with you."

"That would only make him suspicious. Besides, someone ought to alert the police. And we know better than to try to distract Monet. Please, Marcel. I'm afraid if I don't go down there, he'll just take Monet's painting and leave."

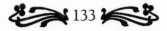

"That might not be such a bad idea—at least you'd be safe." Marcel ran his hand through his hair, a gesture I recognized as pure exasperation. "Oh, Paris. Sometimes I think you ought to take up lion taming. I've never met anyone so bound and determined to walk straight into danger."

"Well," I told him, "at least I've got a good friend who walks right in there with me."

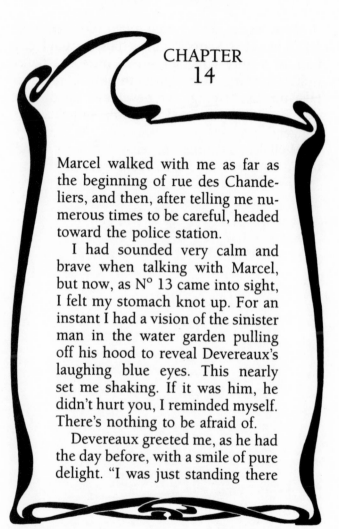

CHAPTER
14

Marcel walked with me as far as the beginning of rue des Chandeliers, and then, after telling me numerous times to be careful, headed toward the police station.

I had sounded very calm and brave when talking with Marcel, but now, as N° 13 came into sight, I felt my stomach knot up. For an instant I had a vision of the sinister man in the water garden pulling off his hood to reveal Devereaux's laughing blue eyes. This nearly set me shaking. If it was him, he didn't hurt you, I reminded myself. There's nothing to be afraid of.

Devereaux greeted me, as he had the day before, with a smile of pure delight. "I was just standing there

looking at the sketch and thinking, She won't come back," he confessed. "I thought I'd scared you off with my terrible temper."

"No—" I halfheartedly started to protest.

"I know, I know—you keep your word." He bowed, ushering me inside.

"Just remember I'm an amateur," I told him.

He handed me the bag again, and I went into the little room to change. The familiar blue of the dress sent a jolt through me—Devereaux might not be a first-rate painter, but he could certainly match color with the best.

"I wish I had a mirror here for you," Devereaux said as I emerged in costume. "You think it looks horrible, but it is really very pretty. It makes you look so . . . innocent."

I took my place in the chair and watched him set up. He was wearing the same dark burgundy jacket as yesterday, only today he had a green scarf around his neck. I forced myself to picture him dressed all in black. He was certainly about the right height, and . . . why hadn't I seen it clearly before? He had a strong, muscular body, not what you'd expect from a man who spent his days wielding a paintbrush. The farm, I thought. He had told me he'd grown up working on a farm.

Mostly to calm my nerves, I asked, "How did a farm boy like you come to be a painter?"

He gave me that infectious smile. "I hated farm work. When I was seventeen, just a little older

than you, I decided that I wasn't going to spend every day wearing myself to the bone so I could get up at dawn the next morning and do it all over again."

"So you decided to become a rich painter like Monet?"

He laughed. "I didn't even know what a painter was then. . . . Tilt your head, please. But I ran away and about three days later realized I didn't have any money, and I didn't know how to do anything except work fields and care for farm animals. So I apprenticed myself to a country veterinarian who did rather well. And what he did with his money was buy paintings. Nothing grand, mind you. Works by unknowns. Still, he had a good eye, and I was entranced! I used to look at those paintings for hours. Finally he noticed and bought me a box of watercolors and a pad. That lit the fire. I stayed with him and painted in my free time till I'd saved enough money to come to Giverny."

"And how long have you been here?" I asked.

"Too long," he said shortly. "Your arm, Paris."

I shifted back into position with a sigh. To be honest, I didn't know how much longer I could continue this charade. The longer I watched Devereaux, the more sure I was that he was the saboteur. And yet, I realized with irritation, he'd charmed me all over again. I didn't want Devereaux to be guilty of anything. I liked him.

At about the point when my arm had gone

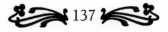

soundly to sleep and I thought it might fall off and drop to the floor, Devereaux called for a break.

"Good," I said, standing up. And then, before he could stop me, I headed for the middle door. "I'm just going to get some water," I called out. "Be right back."

The kitchen was not barren as the other rooms had been. On the contrary, it was absolute chaos. I could barely take in everything that was there—a fireplace with a huge stack of firewood beside it, a veritable mountain of unwashed pots and pans, boxes on the floor out of which clothing spilled, a table and chairs, and on the table, a stack of glass photographic plates.

"Please." Devereaux took me by the arm and steered me firmly back into the main room. "I would rather you let me get you the water. You'd never find a glass in there, I assure you." His voice was light, but from the way he gripped me, there was no mistaking his anger. And that, more than anything else, convinced me I was on to something.

As he disappeared back into the kitchen I went deliberately to the canvases stacked against the wall. There was the one of the train station on top, and behind it a view of the hotel, and another of the village square.

And then there were the Monets. At least a dozen of them, paintings I could swear I'd seen hanging in the second studio that morning. They

were all scenes of the water garden painted when the light was gentlest. Pastel lavenders and blues filled the canvases. Except for one—the very last. All shadow and darkness, it was the missing painting of the water garden, Monet's own foreshadowing of death.

I whirled as the kitchen door opened. Devereaux stood framed in the doorway, my glass of water in his hand. There was an odd expression on his face—a mixture of fury and genuine regret. He spoke softly. "You just couldn't let it alone, could you, Paris?"

CHAPTER
15

He spoke calmly. "Put the painting down."

I did as I was told.

"Good." Very deliberately he raised the water glass above his head and smashed it to the floor. For a moment we both watched as the water streamed across the uneven floorboards. Then he stooped, picked up a jagged shard of glass, and came toward me.

"No," I told him, backing away. "I . . . I just wanted to see your other paintings."

"And now you have. What did you think, Paris? My technique is improving. Perhaps I will be the next Monet."

"You mean maybe you'll *steal* the

next Monet." I jumped as my back hit the wall. I'd literally backed myself into a corner. Devereaux was on me in one lithe move, the sharp edge of the glass against my throat.

"Now walk very slowly back to the chair," he ordered. "And for the record, only one of those is stolen—yes, the one you were holding. The rest are not Monet's, though I did borrow from the great master."

"Borrow? What do you intend to do—give them back?"

"They have already been returned," he said, pushing me down into the chair.

And then I understood. "They're copies," I said slowly. "Forgeries!"

"Perfect forgeries," he corrected me. "They were made from photographs of the originals, which were borrowed from the master with the help of my late friend Antoine." He pressed the glass against my throat, and I felt it cut my skin. "Hold out your hands," he said, "wrists together, straight in front of you." Clasping my wrists with one hand, he tied them tightly with the silk scarf from his neck. Then he pulled a rope out of his jacket pocket and quickly bound me to the chair.

"You killed him," I said. "You killed Antoine."

He shrugged. "Antoine and I had a business arrangement. . . . You will never say anything about this, Paris, will you? No, I will see to that. . . . Then I will tell you. Antoine would borrow the Monets one at a time. I then did color studies, photographed the painting, and copied it. When the forgery was finished, Antoine returned the original, and I would sell the fake. Antoine always got a fair percentage."

"It sounds perfectly harmless," I said sarcastically. "How is it that Antoine wound up dead?"

He smiled, and said as if he were a host talking to a guest, "I'll be with you in a minute. Wait right here." He disappeared into the kitchen and quickly emerged with a large black valise. He brought this over to the wall and, one by one, began laying the paintings in the valise. He was moving very slowly now, holding each painting up to the light, as if savoring it before placing it in the valise.

"On the evening before you arrived," he went on somewhat absently, "Antoine came to pick up a painting so that he could return it to Monet's studio. He told me he'd had a change of heart, that if I didn't destroy the copies, he'd confess everything to Monet." Devereaux turned to look at me for the first time since he'd begun packing. "You must understand, Paris, I now had over a dozen Monets, enough to keep me comfortable for the rest of my life. I had to stop Antoine. I want you to understand this—for it is the reason I must also stop you." He'd packed all but one painting, which he now put aside as he came toward me.

"What are you going to do?" I asked.

"Leave Giverny, assume a new name, set up

my easel far from here, and paint with no financial worries—"

"I meant with me!"

"Shhh . . ." He ran a hand gently down the side of my face. "It's a shame. I've become fond of you." He sighed. "Why did you come here today? I never thought you would. Why did you have to be so suspicious—and so clever?"

"I wasn't that clever," I said angrily. "I was stupid enough to like you!"

He looked at me thoughtfully. "You are too beautiful to meet the same fate as Antoine. I do not think I could hit you."

"That's very kind," I said as calmly as I could. "But I assure you, if you slit my wrists, no one would ever consider it suicide. Not for a minute."

He waved his hand impatiently. "It was not even a good idea for Antoine. I realized that after I'd dragged his body to the water garden. And that's when I decided it was time for the Giverny saboteur to return."

"You would have let some poor villager be tried for murder?"

His dazzling smile sent chills racing through me. "I would not have been here to stop it. Now—what will I do with you?"

"Why did you go back to the second studio for the last Monet?" I asked desperately. "Do you intend to return that one also?"

He looked at the one canvas he had not yet

packed, the painting of the water garden in shade.

"That one, no. It's very important that I have an original Monet for myself." He turned to me and said, "I love him, you know."

I knew then that he was insane, and kept silent. For what could I say to such madness?

As I watched, Devereaux packed the Monet, fastened the valise, and went into the kitchen. A moment later I heard the sound of glass breaking once again.

"A most unfortunate accident," he announced, emerging from the kitchen. "The oil lamp's fallen over."

"You won't get away with this," I said. Then, out of pure panic, I tried to bluff him. "We were in the second studio this morning. We saw that the painting was missing. Monet knows about you."

Devereaux considered this information. "Then I shall stop Monet as well. *Adieu*, Paris." He stooped and kissed me gently. "Perhaps the flames will not hurt you." Then he was gone, locking the door behind him.

I could smell the smoke already. It would not be long before it would spread from the kitchen. I struggled to get free, but it was useless. Devereaux had done an expert job with the rope. "Help!" I screamed, hoping that someone passing on the street would hear me. I screamed until black clouds of smoke began rolling out

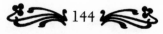

from under the kitchen door.

Then I noticed the broken glass Devereaux had threatened me with. Could I cut the rope with it? The shards lay scattered on the floor, halfway across the room. I jerked my body forward and managed to stand upright, but my ankles were bound so tightly that I couldn't walk forward at all. Then I discovered that it was just possible for me to shift sideways, inch by painful inch, like a crab.

The smoke was now so thick I could barely see. I lost my balance and toppled over with a crash, which turned out to be a very good thing, as it kept my head closer to the floor where it was easier to breathe.

I was trying to pull myself across the floor when a window smashed open, and I heard what sounded like someone launching himself through it.

"Paris!" shouted a familiar voice. "Where are you?"

I tried to shout back, but a fit of coughing was the best I could do. It was enough. Before I knew it, Marcel was at my side, cutting through the rope.

I don't know how he did it, for he was choking nearly as badly as I, but he managed to carry me out onto the street. And there we stood, very unsteadily indeed, coughing uncontrollably, our eyes streaming with tears.

"Well, well," said Marcel as a car appeared at

the end of the rue des Chandeliers. "For the better part of an hour I have been pleading with the police to arrest Devereaux. And all they could say was they'd have to check with Monet first to see if the painting was really missing. But now here come the *gendarmes de Giverny*."

Sure enough, Sergeant Houlbeque, with Henri sitting next to him, was drawing up in the official police auto.

"Are you two all right?" asked the sergeant. "We came as soon as we smelled the smoke."

Marcel turned on him furiously, but before he could say anything, I stepped in front of him, remembering what I'd all but forgotten in the confusion of the fire. "We're fine. But Devereaux said he was going after Monet. He may be at the house by now!"

We all piled into the car, and Sergeant Houlbeque took off for the Maison du Pressoir. Actually, "took off" is misleading. We chugged along at about the pace of an alert cow. If Marcel and I hadn't still had lungs full of smoke, we could have walked to the *Maison* in better time.

Although we'd last seen Monet in the orchard, Sergeant Houlbeque insisted we stop at the house first, where a maid answered the door.

"Monsieur Monet is not in," she replied to Henri's question.

"Well, where is he?" demanded Houlbeque.

"In the water garden, monsieur, but he must not be disturbed!"

"We'll take separate routes," Houlbeque ordered. "Paris, you and Marcel enter the water garden from the entrance closest to the *Maison*. Henri and I will take the car around the property to the other side of the bridge."

So it was that the four of us wound up in the water garden. Unsurprisingly, Marcel and I arrived first. Sergeant Houlbeque and Henri, only a few minutes behind us, stationed themselves on the other side of the bridge. And what we saw was Monet and Devereaux standing at the very midpoint of the bridge. Monet was leaning backward over the railing, and Devereaux had a knife to his throat.

CHAPTER
16

"You think you are so extraordinary," Devereaux was saying to a bewildered Monet. "The founding father of Impressionism! Let me tell you, I have duplicated your masterpieces in an evening's work. So much for your famous technique! You are nothing but a selfish old—"

"That's enough, Devereaux!" shouted Sergeant Houlbeque, his gun drawn. "Very slowly you will drop the knife into the water."

Devereaux never took his eyes off Monet. He leaned over him so that the knife in his fist was wedged between his chest and Monet's throat. "If you shoot me, I will collapse," he said calmly, "and

147

this knife will be driven straight into Monsieur Monet's throat. Consider that well, Monsieur Houlbeque."

"And why couldn't you have had the courtesy to at least look at my work?" he demanded of Monet. "It's not as if I begged free lessons. I just wanted you to look. You don't know how hard I worked to come here. But you don't care. You—"

"I—" Monet tried to answer, but there was no reasoning with Devereaux. He turned the knife so that its full blade, not just the point, lay across Monet's throat. Monet's legs began to shake.

I couldn't take it any longer. Without even knowing I was doing it, I screamed out, "Devereaux, please stop!"

He did stop, long enough to turn and stare at me, wild-eyed.

"Paris!" he said. "You are alive! How in heaven's name . . . ?"

With a surge of energy Monet twisted free and wrested the knife away from Devereaux. And for the first time I saw Devereaux frightened. With a cry of pure terror he leaped from the bridge into the shallow waters below.

Quickly Sergeant Houlbeque and Henri waded in and dragged him from the water. As they handcuffed him he stared at me.

"Paris!" he cried. "I knew the flames would not hurt you."

"Come along now," said Sergeant Houlbeque,

slapping him on the shoulder. "Let's not have any trouble." As they led him away Devereaux looked back. With a pathetic shadow of his old smile he called out, "Paris, I'm glad you're still alive, and still so beautiful. I wish . . . no. This time, I fear, it really is *adieu.*"

He was right. I never saw him again.

"So Devereaux actually was the saboteur," Mme. Monet said.

"The irises, the letter, the water lilies—they were all ruses to draw suspicion away from himself," I explained.

We were taking a leisurely walk around the water garden. We'd had a pretty hectic day since Devereaux's arrest, what with police interviews, an examination of the second studio, and a return to the charred ruins of Antoine's house. But at last Jean-Pierre had gone to the *gendarmerie* to tie up the remaining official business, and the Monets had invited us out for a stroll around the grounds.

Now we were ambling along the path by the south side of the lily pool, where irises grew down to the water's edge on our right, and lovely peony bushes, bedecked with white and crimson flowers, banked up to our left. The sun, pink and hazy, was setting low in the sky in front of us, and there was a sweet, fresh scent in the air, the fragile scent of a spring evening, mild and a little misty. It was very peaceful.

Monet and Marcel walked some way ahead, deep in conversation. We were almost back to the bridge now—to the very spot where I'd had my first, unforgettable meeting with Monet. How long ago it seemed!

"Madame," I said, "I've been so curious. Would you tell me why you fired Antoine, and why you didn't tell anyone the reason?"

Mme. Monet sighed. "That morning I'd gone up to the second studio to get a painting for Monet's agent; he had a buyer for one of the landscapes. And I found Antoine in the studio. He held a portfolio, like artists use, and he was taking one of Monet's paintings out of it.

"Antoine had always done decent work for us, and I thought he was a good man. I couldn't believe what I was seeing! You may think me foolish, Paris, but I didn't ask any questions. I told him to leave this house and never return. . . . As for not telling anyone—he looked so stricken when I found him that I had no wish to disgrace him further. I told him this would be kept between the two of us."

I smiled. I'd come to like Alice Monet more and more. "You weren't that far wrong," I said, and explained how Antoine had tried to stop Devereaux.

"And so he died," she finished quietly, her face gone pale. "I do not think anyone's paintings are worth a life. It is tragic that he became involved with Devereaux—but I'm glad to know that I did not misjudge him."

Ahead of us, Marcel and Monet stopped, shook hands as if they'd just arrived at some agreement, and waited for us to catch up with them. Both of them were beaming.

"I wonder what those two have been hatching?" Mme. Monet said.

As we approached, Monet cleared his throat.

"My dear Paris," he began—Mme. Monet had told him to stop saying "mademoiselle," and he'd told me I could call him "Monet"—"my dear Paris, I've asked Marcel what I can possibly do to express my gratitude to both of you. No, no, don't you dare argue—that's an order! Devereaux never would have been caught if it weren't for you. Marcel has given the matter a lot of thought, and he's finally decided that an ideal gift would be a painting by me."

"Oh. But I couldn't—" I began.

"Not just any old painting, mind you," Monet continued. "A specially commissioned one. A portrait—of you."

I was overwhelmed—and a little dismayed—at the prospect of having to model again, even for Monet.

All I could do was stare open-mouthed as Monet went on. "There is, however, a snag. Portraits are hardly my forté—at least, not portraits that are painted in studios. I'm afraid you'll have to spend quite a lot of time here in the garden, posing." He paused to adjust his vest, then continued with mock solemnity. "Your stay here will have to be extended by a fortnight at least. I'm sorry, but it can't be helped. . . ." Suddenly he burst into great peals of laughter, and I knew Marcel had told him how bad I was at posing.

"I'd love to stay," I said, "but my parents are coming to Paris on July 4, for my birthday. I have to go back."

"How like you," Monet said, "to be born on your country's Independence Day. . . . Very well, if you refuse my invitation, I shall have to offer it again. Would you come at the end of the summer?" He turned to Marcel. "With a friend, of course."

"It would be my pleasure," I told him.

"And mine," said Marcel.

"Then it's settled." Alice Monet leaned against her husband's shoulder, and there was a spark of mischief in her eyes. "And every day, Paris, after you have finished modeling, you and I will go driving!"

How different the Monets were now from the way they'd been when we first met them. Alice, in that moment, was young again; and Monet, on the selfsame spot where he'd grumpily threatened to throw us off his property, was as merry as the Santa Claus he so resembled.

"Well, Alice," he said at last, "I think we'd better be making our way back to the house, eh? It won't be long till dinner, and there's plenty

for us to do. I'm sure our young friends would like some time to themselves. . . ."

"Yes, Monet, I quite agree," she said. "Well, now, Paris and Marcel, we shall see you later. I do hope you'll enjoy the rest of your stay with us."

Monet raised his hand and waved; then the two of them linked arms and walked away over the bridge, closing the green door behind them.

Marcel drew me close, and together we walked up onto the bridge. There we stood and gazed out over the pool, which was golden now with the light of dusk. There wasn't a sound to be heard, save the rustling of the leaves and the gentle lapping of the water.

We stood there like that for a while, each of us lost in thought. So much had happened here, and so much had changed. As I watched the play of sunlight and shadow on the water I realized suddenly what it was about Monet's vision that was so special. It was as if he not only saw nature but could penetrate deep into its very heart. And through his paintings he revealed that heart: light and shadow, life and death.

Then softly a voice murmured, "Paris."

I turned and looked into eyes that seemed to understand everything I'd been thinking.

"Yes, Marcel."

And this time, on the green bridge, there was nothing to keep us from kissing.

How long is the dance prog

1 or 1½ hrs